THE CONVENT

SARAH SHERIDAN

BLOODHOUND
— BOOKS —

For my wonderful mother, Sue

'*The more intense has been the religion of any period and the more profound has been the dogmatic belief, the greater has been the cruelty and the worse has been the state of affairs.*'
Bertrand Russell

1

Twenty-four hours before the murder took place, Sister Veronica Angelica leaned forward over her desk, her head cocked sideways. She was editing a thrilling car chase; a scene that rode the arc of chapter fourteen in her latest crime story beautifully. Blissfully unaware of the darkness that awaited her, the only distraction hampering her creation of a suitable climax was the incessant hammering from next door.

BANG! BANG! CRASH!

She threw down her pen and thumped the desk with her fist. Saints preserve her, did those builders not realise she only had twenty minutes before afternoon prayers began? How a nun was expected to write a book under these conditions she did not know. Aware that her trusted friend and proofreader, Sister Agnes Claire, was keen to see the finished manuscript, Sister Veronica had an insatiable desire to complete it, but those builders had been pounding away at the extension to the youth hostel since well before morning prayers. It was terribly off-putting. While extra room at the busy hostel was much needed, and she should know because she worked there three days a week, at this rate she was going to have to wait until after evening mass to finish the chapter. Which was *such* a shame as she had been so looking forward to penning the moment Father Dominic discovered his housekeeper's body in the back of a burnt-out car.

Her train of thought now disrupted, Sister Veronica squinted through the window at the vibrant street life of London's Soho Square Gardens, her sharp green eyes taking in the sunbathers on the fenced-in square of patchy grass, the smiling couples walking hand in hand, the Japanese tourists with their cameras and the troop of Hare Krishna followers weaving a lively passage through everyone else. All the activity took place theatre-like amid the set of a quadrangle of historic four-storey buildings; the view was definitely Sister Veronica's favourite for people-watching. She felt an air of light expectancy pervading the streets, matching the warmer-than-usual spring climate, and she exhaled, smiling. But the sight of a scuttling tall, brown-haired man wearing a dog collar and advancing towards her building prompted her eyebrows to lower, as she remembered who was taking afternoon prayers in the Convent of the Christian Heart that day.

Sighing, she wondered if she was the only one to dislike Father Mathers. His slippery eye contact, habit of listening at doors, and questionable comments about anyone who didn't fit his idea of middle class and above, made him an unsavoury compatriot. Yet so many of the other sisters seemed to adore him, and his clever sermons had them talking for days. Sister Veronica knew she mustn't let on that she didn't like the man, people were too close for comfort in her world and word would get back to him. She had no plans to draw attention to herself, not after last time. It had all been most unpleasant and eyes had been on her for weeks; creeping away for murder-mystery writing had become nearly impossible.

Taking a deep breath, Sister Veronica shut her notebook and

stood up. Catching sight of her reflection in the window she chuckled. Well, well, well, it looked like she'd put on a few more pounds. She saw that some wisps of her grey hair, pulled back in a sensible bun that morning, had come loose and hung round her face. For a moment she was transported back to her childhood, when, despite her mother's best efforts to tame them, locks of her then red hair had continually escaped as she galloped through the fields of her parents' Sussex farm. Memories of the terrible moment she'd found out her adored parents weren't all that they seemed flashed by, and her heart began its usual pounding.

Feeling her eyes moisten, she shook her head. Now now, we'll have none of that, thank you, she told herself. Good grief, there's no time for baby tears. Not when that priest's mutterings have to be endured with passable grace.

Smoothing down her long tweed skirt and wishing her supposedly loose-fitting blouse wasn't pinching quite so tightly, Sister Veronica opened her bedroom door. Now keep that temper of yours under control, she told herself sternly, stepping out into the bare corridor. Even if he says the most trying things, don't react. No trouble, not again. It makes writing so very difficult, and that just won't do. Kneel quietly, reflect on your vows, pray for the poor and think of how best to end the chapter.

Adopting her customary rolling gait, and heading through the double doors and towards the staircase, Sister Veronica brushed her blouse downwards in case any stray crumbs had stayed behind after her early afternoon snack. Custard creams did aid the writing process, she found. As she lumbered slowly down the stairs, she could hear bedroom doors opening and closing, a variety of footsteps getting louder behind her; the motley crew of seven other sisters who shared life in the convent were also on their way.

Sister Veronica was just reflecting on how, being two floors up, she did quite a lot of exercise on a daily basis, what with all the mealtimes and prayers and masses held on the ground floor, when she saw a bob of bright blonde hair through the window of the fire door on the first floor.

'Oh dash,' she murmured, as the door swung open, and a young lady fell into step with her.

'All right, Sister Veronica?' the young lady said, her husky South London accent still unfamiliar within the convent walls; not grating exactly – almost exotic – a reminder of other worlds and lives. Her eyes sought out the nun's; the startling keenness and drive in them contrasting with the customary dissociation Sister Veronica saw in many of her sisters' eyes.

'Oh hello, Melissa, what a pleasant surprise,' Sister Veronica said, giving the young journalist a once-over. Apart from exchanging pleasantries at mealtimes, she'd so far successfully avoided talking to this attractive imposter who'd burst into their quiet religious life three days ago. She had to look upwards to take in the girl's angular, bronzed face with its wide green eyes, which was framed by a bob of wavy, dyed blonde hair smattered with fading pink highlights. Sister Veronica instinctively pulled her spine in, drawing herself up to her maximum possible height of five feet three inches, then glanced over at Melissa to see if she'd gained anything on her.

Typically, it had been Father Mathers who had been interested when *Women of the World* magazine emailed him, asking if he knew any sisters who would be happy to have a reporter living with them for a week to find out 'what life was really like as a nun'. He'd gone to some lengths to persuade the Mother Superior that it would be a sensible idea to allow the journalist to stay at the convent. Another way of building good community links, he'd said. Maybe he'd seen a photo of Melissa Carlton prior to his enthusiasm, Sister Veronica had speculated, before pushing the thought into the very private 'not for public consumption' section of her brain.

Melissa threw Sister Veronica a wide smile, flashing a row of large white teeth, a wide gap between the front two.

'Prayer time is so peaceful, isn't it?' the girl said. Yes, still a girl, Sister Veronica was sure she couldn't be a day over twenty-six. 'I don't often get a chance to stop and think in my normal life, but I've thought more over the last few days than I have all year.'

'Yes. Quite.' Sister Veronica did indeed find prayers and mass very peaceful times. She fervently believed in a higher power greater than all humankind, but Father Mather's subtly prejudiced sermons made her brain overheat, and she didn't think God would mind if she tuned those bits out in favour of ruminating on her next chapter. Also, after having been a sister for over thirty-eight years, which was arguably a long time for anyone to enjoy near-constant meditation on Catholic dogma and discipline, Vatican II and the uproarious news events that had dogged the Roman Catholic Church throughout the twenty-first century, Sister Veronica couldn't help but see a chasm-like difference between what she sensed was there spiritually, and the human-made world of religion; which at times – and she was sorry but this was the truth – was nothing but trouble. She hadn't lost her faith, no, not at all. The fact was she'd developed her own simple belief, a pact of love between the greater power of the multiverse and herself, and that was who she prayed to. The militant Catholic rule-keepers and dogma enthusiasts who loved to tell people they were wrong all the time had to be borne with a detached patience. The problem was, as Sister Veronica frequently reflected, she wasn't very good at detached patience and constantly had to bite down the urge to tell them exactly what she thought of them.

'I'm glad I've caught you actually,' Melissa said, stopping and waiting at the bottom of the staircase for Sister Veronica to roll down the last few steps. 'I've been hoping we could arrange to have a quick chat at some point, whenever suits you really?'

Sister Veronica Angelica sighed inwardly. She'd had an inkling this question was coming; over the last few days she'd watched four of her other sisters peel off from communal activities to have nice cosy chats with Melissa in the garden or the lobby.

'All right,' she replied, puffing a bit as she reached the ground floor, the heavy wooden cross she wore round her neck swinging from side to side. 'How about during reading time, before dinner? I'll have to check with Mother Superior but I don't think she'll mind. We can take a walk in the garden, perhaps.' Sister Veronica had no intention of going up all those stairs to her room again, not until after evening prayers.

'Perfect, that works well for me.' Melissa's eyes darted around, watching the nuns descend the stairs one by one and head for the chapel.

'Right, then.' Sister Veronica waited by the stairs, hoping that now she'd succumbed to Melissa's wishes, the young journalist would leave her alone. She'd become so used to the quietness in the convent that she found talking too much within its walls intrusive, especially to people she hardly knew. It was different next door in the youth hostel, of course, that was a place designed for socialising; the atmosphere was alive and dynamic, and chatting was a necessary part of that. But here in the convent the near silence was sacred.

Melissa seemed to get the hint, and smiled before walking off. But then she stopped and turned.

'You won't forget, will you?' she asked, her eyes betraying her, a hint of something in them suddenly – now what was it – desperation? Fear? Sister Veronica caught her breath in astonishment, then shook her head. If the girl's presence in the convent held a meaning beyond the act of journalism, she had no intention of finding out what it was. Any hint of trouble, as far as she was concerned, could stay very far away from her indeed.

Dawdling in the stairwell to give Melissa a good head start into the chapel, she nodded to the last of her comrades to descend the stairs; Sister Maria, a shy novice who was still in the first flush of religious ideation.

'Are you coming, Sister?' Sister Maria peered at her anxiously. 'We don't want to be late.'

'I'm on my way, Sister. Just resting my sore knee for a minute, you know how it plays up. You go on and I'll follow.' Sister Veronica nodded and ushered the novice away with her hands. She was fond of Sister Maria, and wondered, vaguely, why the enthusiastic young novice was the last one down to prayers when she was usually one of the first.

Her mind slipped back to her chapter, she knew there was an idea there just waiting to be teased to the surface. All she needed was a bit of peace to encourage it and she fully intended to kneel near the back, as this was her best thinking place. Watching Sister Maria's back view disappear, she walked slowly towards the chapel, past the kitchen door that was pulled to. A smell of boiled milk from lunchtime's rice pudding hung in the air, mingling with the sharp odours of cleaning products. From inside the kitchen came a low murmuring – two voices. One was a man's voice. Father Mathers, she thought, surprised. Why isn't he already in chapel? And who's he talking to? Sister Veronica didn't mean to listen, not really. It was her bad knee that made her slow down to a halt and sway towards the door.

'No, I haven't done it yet. You'll have to give me more time.' Father Mathers spat each word out in low staccato.

Someone must have responded although Sister Veronica

couldn't hear what was being said or who was saying it. She held her breath.

'I've promised you, haven't I? Now I really must go, or they'll wonder where I am.' He sounded agitated, a far cry from his usual smooth persona. There was the sound of a chair scraping backwards.

With unusual speed, Sister Veronica lunged towards the chapel, dropping heavily into the nearest pew, the impact making her wince. She buried her head in her hands. Numb shock gave way to an angry, rising heat. What was that foolish priest up to? Fighting the instinct to immediately report what she'd heard to Mother Superior or even announce it to the assembled nuns, she remembered her promise to herself to remain inconspicuous and keep out of trouble.

The chapel, the largest ground-floor room in their historic building, had originally been used as a library for the Duke of Sussex. Normally, Sister Veronica liked to imagine the layers of contemplation and reflection that had taken place within its walls over the changing centuries. She knew that King Charles II had the building constructed for his friend, the Duke, in 1677, when Soho Square was quite the fashionable place for aristocracy to live. Now, maintained by Westminster City Council, the building was stripped of any grandeur inside, which Sister Veronica was glad about as she couldn't abide fancy airs and graces. She wholeheartedly believed in her vow of poverty which didn't mean – as a few lay people seemed to think – that religious folk promised to live in abject destitution. It was more about all possessions belonging with equal weight to each member of the community, and living with gratitude and modesty; Sister Veronica suspected that this Western fascination with capitalism could learn a thing or two from it.

But there was no time for historical rumination today, it was all she could do to slow her breaths and hope that the pulsating angry heat in her head and heart wasn't obvious. As she grasped the wooden pew in front for strength, a whoosh of air beside her and the loud tones that followed announced Father Mather's arrival.

'Good sisters.' He projected his educated – now calm – tones around the room. 'Let us bow our heads in prayer as we ask for the grace to answer your call with obedience and love.'

After a few minutes of furious prayer for the continued protection and sanctity of her convent in the face of all wrongdoing, Sister Veronica peered through her fingers and allowed herself a quick glance around. Sister Maria, right at the front, was looking up with no doubt rapt attention at Father Mathers, who now stood behind the altar, his arms spread beneficently outwards, his eyes closing. His robes hung slickly around him and his carefully parted hair remained unruffled. Sister Veronica added 'good actor' to her list of his character traits. Who were you just talking to? Sister Veronica asked him silently. What haven't you done yet? What have you promised? She couldn't and wouldn't look at the man for long in case her thoughts were so loud they drew his attention to her, so she let her hidden gaze pan sideways.

Behind Sister Maria, knelt Sister Agnes Claire, Sister Veronica's best friend at the convent. Her shoulders were sagging, and Sister Veronica suspected that her friend's rheumatism had been keeping her up again so she said a quick prayer, asking for Sister Agnes's pain be taken away. The cold British climate was a far cry from her friend's birth place of Kerala state in south-western India, and rheumatic pain had dogged her since her arrival in London eighteen years previously. Sister Veronica wondered whether to relay the overheard conversation to Sister Agnes at some point.

Turning her head a fraction to the right, she saw Melissa kneeling further down her pew, the fear in her eyes now gone but the look on her face unreadable as she stared straight ahead. On the other side of Melissa was Mother Superior, Sister Julia Augusta. Her eyes were closed and her lined face as sternly pious as usual. Mother Superior always arrived fifteen minutes before every prayer session and mass, typically sinking to her knees with histrionic zeal and staying rigidly still until ten minutes after each session had finished. Sister Veronica felt this exaggerated obeisance to the powers that be might be slightly overdoing it, but who was she to comment. Mother Superior had been at the convent for forty-three years and was the longest practising sister, yet no one knew much about her at all. Discussing one's previous life wasn't encouraged as it apparently distracted a nun from fully giving herself over to God, and each sister adhered to this in greater or lesser ways; some were naturally more open, and everyone knew everything about jolly Sister Catherine's former life and was all the better for it, in Sister Veronica's opinion.

Sister Catherine, still a relative newcomer by convent standards, had arrived from Australia the year before. A ruddy-faced natural extrovert, she loved to talk and often kept Sister Veronica entertained with tales from her parents' outback farm during mealtimes. Sister Veronica couldn't see her or her two other sisters, they must be kneeling in the pews behind her and she couldn't very well turn her head round to stare, which was vexing as she liked to keep an eye on everything that was going on.

On second thoughts, it was probably for the best as the last thing she wanted to do was make eye contact with Sister Irene, whose role as Assistant Superior made her second in command at the convent. Although the nuns elected Mother and Assistant Superiors every five years, and the nuns undertaking these roles were still meant to be equals to the rest of the sisters in the convent, Sister Veronica often suspected that Sister Irene hadn't received that important bit of information. A ferocious rule-keeper and dogma enthusiast, Sister Irene looked sourly on Sister Veronica's mild rebellious tendencies to think for herself and took every opportunity to get her in trouble. She must be sitting with old Sister Anastasia, who tended to drift off during longer masses, and Sister Mary Pemii who was in the midst of a six month visit from a Convent of the Christian Heart in Nigeria.

Risking a peek towards Father Mathers, she saw the priest's eyes were now wide open. He was staring straight at her, a strange look on his face. She had a sudden thought that he'd seen her walking away from the kitchen and had realised she'd overheard his conversation. Maybe she'd been too slow, maybe her footsteps had been too loud. Intentionally keeping her face as mild and blank as possible, her heart rate quickened and a small thrill of rage ricocheted through her. Why should she be feeling guilty for walking through her own home? It wasn't right. It wouldn't do at all. She bowed her head downwards, and said a prayer for all those with deceitful intent, asking that they may live with honesty and without guile.

After several minutes, she raised her eyes. Father Mather's eyes had closed again, his hands pressed together as though in deep prayer.

Now calm down, she counselled herself. The angry heat inside her ebbed a bit, and Sister Veronica wondered whether she'd read more into the encounter than was really there. Was it possible that she'd let her personal dislike for Father Mathers colour her judgement? It wouldn't be the first time. Perhaps it was an innocent promise not yet fulfilled, such as paying the gardener, or counselling a seminarian, it wouldn't surprise her if it was that tall, young, fair-haired trainee she'd seen trailing after him recently; those two had developed an unusually close bond. Relaxing a little, she heard the front door click into place. Clearly, whoever he'd been speaking to had just left.

Suddenly, the whole peculiar encounter seemed surreal and she felt a little foolish. She didn't like Father Mathers, that was for sure. The problem with clericalism was that it changed some people for the worse. If they didn't live their lives from love and cut themselves off too much from the comfort of human contact it dehumanised them; they became cold, selfish, sometimes unpleasant. She'd seen it happen many times, and Father Mathers fitted the bill perfectly. No one could forget the awful saga with Father Cuthbert; the courts had found him guilty of molesting three altar boys and the shame it brought on the Diocese of Westminster was still tangible. Word among the religious folk was that Cardinal Moore was planning a series of targeted visits around Westminster with the press in tow. While Sister Veronica didn't hold with much of the sensationalist reporting that went on nowadays, she felt anything that raised the profile of good, hard-working priests and nuns would be beneficial.

She sighed. She'd written enough crime fiction – in secret of course, entirely unpublished more's the pity – to know that basing an indictment on one overheard conversation alone was ridiculous. The best thing, she decided, was to ignore the man. She'd forget she ever heard anything and carry on as before. No need to tell Sister Agnes about her experience. It was probably nothing anyway, she told herself. Probably nothing at all.

Closing her eyes, she visualised the next events in her chapter; the car chase, the crash, the burnt-out wreckage, the housekeeper's body. She imagined Sister Agnes's delight and absorption while reading it. Her mind's eye panned slowly onto the housekeeper's face. Suddenly, it changed, metamorphosing into Father Mather's face. His eyes were open, staring at her, a smirk twisting his bulbous features. She shivered and her right hand clasped firmly around her wooden cross.

2

Clearing away the debris from breakfast time, Jamie Markham rolled up his sleeves; yesterday's warm air had turned stickily humid. His bare wrists bore the giant scars from last year's suicide attempt; violent white slashes criss-crossed with the life-saving marks of the surgeon's stitches – a permanent reminder of the night he'd lacerated his arms with the broken glass of a wine bottle. He didn't like people looking at them, but there was no one else nearby; all the other hostel guests had already upped and left the room, most of them already out of the building, doing whatever it was they did during the day.

Cursing the students – and they were mainly students or backpackers with the exception of the old hippie, Jon Barrow – for the bloody mess they made every mealtime (they ate like pigs in his opinion), Jamie felt a pang of satisfaction as he guided each crumb, fragment of egg shell, crust and apple core into a neat pile at the edge of the table. Using his carefully rinsed dishcloth for guidance, he swiped the pile into his hand with mathematical precision, successfully aiming every piece for the centre of his palm with no collateral damage falling to the floor. He admired his own dexterity, then hated himself for admiring it.

Purposefully not looking through the window at the rubble of bricks messing up the garden, Jamie realised that the throbbing in his head had already eased; in fact, it had started to wane the minute he'd read the note he'd found on the doormat at seven that morning written in perfect copperplate swirls; *Builders not coming today, been called to an emergency, should be back over the next couple of days. God bless, Sister Julia.* The incessant bloody banging that had marked each day for two weeks as the workmen knocked down an old wall outside had physically hurt his brain. Since his mother had gone hysterical in the hospital after seeing the stitches criss-crossing his lacerated wrists for the first time, Jamie's thoughts had become physically painful, and each blow of the builders' sledgehammers magnified this pain. Keeping busy was a good distraction from this, and quietness was a balm.

Walking into the kitchen to deposit his handful into the food waste bin, Jamie saw Mark and the new French girl, Celine, chatting near the door to the dining room. They were standing very close together. Celine's low top revealed a generous portion of her firm, tanned breasts and Jamie wished it was him talking to her instead of Mark.

Turning away before they saw him, Jamie brought his attention back to today's main task. He'd identified which of the nuns from next door's convent he was going to tell his secret to – he'd chosen that large-faced one, Sister Veronica, as she reminded him of his grandmother; she actually listened when he talked, she didn't just disengage from people in the sanctimonious way some of the other sisters did – now he just needed to work out how and when to orchestrate the conversation. He'd have to choose a moment when her friend, that old busybody, Father John, wasn't around. They usually turned up within an hour of each other.

It was imperative that he got the conditions just right, everything he wanted to do and all the action he wanted to take, depended on Sister Veronica's help. He knew that what had happened to him all those years ago wasn't right, but he still found it very difficult to talk about. But he must, he must. The bottled-up anger was killing him.

It had been an impulse to arrange a stay at the Catholic Youth Hostel two months previously. Jamie knew a connection to Westminster Diocese was important to establish if he was going to achieve what he wanted to, but he'd struggled to know how to initiate it. Googling the area, he'd come across the Convent of the Christian Heart and the hostel they ran. A short phone call later, Jamie found himself on the train from Sidcup, the sleepy Kent suburb where his mum lived, to London's Victoria Station the next day, his modest savings transferred to his current account. He was an artist, he'd said to the nuns who'd welcomed him, studying at Kensington College of Art and Design, and needed somewhere to stay. Which wasn't a complete lie, was it? His cover story held many elements of truth. He'd been to art college for a year and seven months, albeit in Bromley not Kensington. The suicide attempt and its aftermath had ground his fine art project on Impressions of Horror to an abrupt halt, but the nuns didn't need to know that detail. Anyway, he knew what he had to do here was more important than creating coagulating blood effects on canvas with acrylic paint. He'd found his true calling, and by following it he would be repairing some of the damage done to him.

Just thinking about the importance of his plan caused Jamie's heart to beat faster, dizziness to flood his brain. He'd been prone to panic attacks since he'd read that letter two months ago, and he hated himself for being so weak. Leaning against the sink, he tried to regulate his breaths, and commended himself for the calm feeling that washed through his body. Then he hated himself for his own vanity. Then he hated all the people; the priests, his mother, his fucking teachers, who'd drip-fed him the idea that vanity, that anything for that matter, was a sin. Fucking Catholic bullshit. Jamie knew from experience that Catholicism was a cult, and that he was one of its victims. But not for much longer.

The sight of a knife covered in strawberry jam lying on a plate nearby jolted his increasingly obsessive mind. He mustn't let his standards slip; he'd felt honoured when Sister Catherine, after guessing that he was struggling with money, had suggested he swap his housekeeping abilities for a vastly reduced room fee. He washed up the remaining breakfast clutter with a thoroughness Sister Veronica had commended on many occasions. The two of them had become quite close, Jamie thought. He'd often found her staring at him intently, not unkindly, just with an absorbed interest, and he'd come to the conclusion that maybe he reminded her of a brother or nephew from long ago.

Drying each bowl, side plate, spoon and knife until any hint of moisture had been meticulously removed, Jamie heard voices, a carefree laugh – Celine's, he thought – then the opening and closing of the front door. The last of the hostel's guests had left. He paused, realising Mark and Celine had left together. Then he exhaled, relieved at the sudden solitude. It was Sister Veronica's day to visit the hostel, Jamie had memorised her timetable a couple of weeks ago. Always a stickler for punctuality, she would arrive at half past three on the dot, armed with ingredients for today's teatime cake. He would offer to help her make it. It would be the perfect time for him to disclose his secret to her, before the hustle and bustle of the returning rabble ruined their time together.

A scraping noise in the backyard jolted him from his thoughts. What was that? Probably a bird or a cat. There was enough rubbish out there these days to entertain a whole army of bored wildlife. A tepid breeze wafted over his arms. He must have left the back door open, he thought. He'd got into the habit of doing that due to those bloody builders usually going in and out all day. Placing the last gleaming knife carefully in the correct section in the cutlery drawer, Jamie turned towards the utility room, resolving to investigate the noise. He was unaware that this would be the last decision he would ever make.

3

Sister Veronica tucked her carrier bag under her arm and clutched the banister. It was half past two and a muggy air was pervading the convent. Dressed for the heat in her lightest skirt and shirt, she stomped down the stairs a little louder than was necessary. She wouldn't have admitted to this for one minute, but combined with her tired agitation was a sense of aliveness; a part of her that had been asleep for years had woken up. It had been that conversation yesterday with the girl, Melissa, that had done it, on top of yesterday's strange goings-on. What with having a penchant for creating mysteries through writing, there was something curiously thrilling about being involved with something unexplained oneself.

At first, sitting in the garden with the young journalist in the sultry afternoon sun, Sister Veronica had been impatient. She'd wanted to get the meeting done and over with as soon as possible; she missed the peace that writing gave her. The girl was likeable enough, even if she did have a rather loose dress sense. There was something elegant about the way she carried herself, and it must have taken some pluckiness to have immersed herself in the unique convent setting, after all, it was not something that was usually possible for outsiders. But she didn't really see what either party could gain from what was sure to be a superficial chat, what could she possibly say that would interest her? They'd both chosen different life paths, they had vastly different ways of living, why couldn't they just both get on with going about their business, instead of pretending that some cultural value would emerge from a ten-minute interaction? Remember your vows, Veronica, she told herself. For once just be obedient without making such a fuss.

Melissa had stared out over the small yellowing lawn for a good few seconds. The scent of dry grass had hung around them, as still as the air. The girl had sat straight-backed, a beaded kaftan flowing over her bronzed limbs, her slim legs – clad in long white leggings – neatly crossed. Sister Veronica had found herself staring at the girl's sandals, which were dark bronze in colour with light and dark beads threaded over the straps. They were strangely fascinating. But she'd remembered something her mother had told her many years ago, that it was rude to stare at someone's shoes as it made you come across as disdainful, so she forced her gaze away and adopted a look of patient beneficence until the girl was ready to talk.

'Sister Veronica,' Melissa had begun in her gravelly tones. 'Thank you so much for taking the time to talk to me, I really do appreciate it. If you feel comfortable with this, could you tell me a bit about what led up to your decision to enter a convent?'

With an internal sigh, this was exactly the sort of question she'd predicted Melissa would ask, Sister Veronica elaborated on how she was brought up in a devout Catholic family, how she'd always felt an affinity with the sisters who'd taught her in school, and how she'd felt called to be a nun because she felt most herself when she was at one with God. There was no point explaining to the girl about how over the years she'd started questioning the way some parts of the Catholic Church worked, and that now she'd made peace with her own private relationship with God, or love, or the universe, or whatever you wanted to call it. Goodness knows the Church had had enough bad press recently, and the last thing it needed was some young journalist twisting her words to sell magazines. And there was absolutely no way she would ever tell Melissa about the awful thing that had happened when she was thirteen, and that part of her decision to become a nun was driven by guilt.

Melissa had pulled out a shiny notebook and had written in large swirly writing while she talked.

'Do you mind if I ask if you ever considered getting married or starting a family before you became a nun?' The girl's eyes had sharpened as she asked this question.

Sister Veronica smiled. If the girl was hoping for some juicy gossip she certainly wouldn't be getting any.

'My dear,' she'd replied, pulling herself up. 'Women who choose to be nuns are still human. Of course we have past lives, some of us have fallen in love with men before, or even had relationships before we took our vows. To know how to love is one of the greatest assets of being a nun. But the trick is knowing that *after* one takes one's vows, one will be able to direct that love in other ways, such as working with the community, which is one of my favourite things to do, why I spend so much time in the hostel next door. My vows of chastity, obedience and poverty are very important to me and I have always kept them, it is my pleasure to do so.' Except obedience, she added to herself. On the odd occasion. After all, to err is human, to forgive is divine.

'It's just...' Melissa began, then stopped. Why did the girl suddenly look troubled? Was she thinking of becoming a nun, and didn't know if she could be celibate? From the way she'd seen Father Mather's young protégé, Father Adams, staring at Melissa, and from the look she'd given him in return, Sister

Veronica felt that whatever the girl's future career involved it certainly wasn't celibacy.

'Yes?' Sister Veronica asked gently, half expecting a confession of some sort.

'There is something else I want to ask you, actually.' In an instant, Melissa seemed to shrink; instead of a glamorous journalist, Sister Veronica suddenly saw a scared child in front of her. 'But...'

'Ask me anything you like.' Sister Veronica chuckled. 'I may be a nun, but I can assure you I'm rarely shocked by anything these days.'

'No, it's not that.' Melissa bit her little fingernail. 'It's just, I don't know if I'm allowed to talk to you about this. I think I better check with my, um, boss, before I ask you.'

'That's absolutely fine, Melissa. Come and find me whenever you're ready and we can continue the conversation.' Sister Veronica stared at the girl, puzzled. Well, this was unexpected. There was clearly something disturbing her but what on earth could that be? Seeing someone so concerned about something but unable to express it tugged exasperatingly at her heart. It was the vulnerability, it made her want to care for the person, to protect them from the world. Their pain became her pain. She was sure a psychologist would have a field day with this, given her own teenage experiences. But no psychologist would ever get the chance, she was sure of that.

Melissa shook her head a little, a dazed expression on her face.

'Thank you,' she said, standing up, and regaining some of her composure. 'You've been very kind. I'll get back to you as soon as I can, when I've had a word with my editor.'

Yesterday, this conversation had seemed intriguing, to the point where Sister Veronica had lost valuable sleeping hours mulling it over. But today it felt vexing. Tantalising snippets just wouldn't do. For goodness' sake, she'd nearly fallen asleep during morning prayers, and lunchtime sitting next to Sister Catherine had been a veritable struggle. On top of that, was the intolerably relentless heat. Running the back of her hand across her damp forehead, she finally arrived on the ground floor and trudged towards the kitchen.

Thankfully, there was no one else there. She could hear murmurings from the garden; Sisters Maria and Mary were probably tending to the sparse beds of flowers. Sometimes they wheeled Sister Anastasia outside. Although nearly blind now, Sister Anastasia did enjoy being in the sun. A look of peace would come over her as she drifted off. She was the last of the nuns to continue wearing her dark-blue habit, wispy strands of hair escaping from its neat folds. Sister Veronica was glad she'd taken hers off twenty years ago, when given the choice. Wearing it in this humidity would have been too much. She hoped Sister Agnes was out in the garden too, the heat would do her rheumatism no end of good.

Dumping her carrier bag on the counter, she retrieved a packet of custard creams from the snack cupboard. Crunching through them, she ferreted around for today's cake ingredients. She wasn't in the right frame of mind for the coffee and walnut one, today's would be a plain jam sponge.

As she finished shoving the last of her requirements into her bag, the sound of the door creaking made her turn.

'Ah. Sister Irene.'

'Hello, Sister. I see you found the custard creams again.' Sister Irene looked down her nose at the empty packet before whisking it away to the recycling bin. 'Why not try an apple next time?'

Sister Veronica stopped what she was doing and peered up at the tall, sour-faced nun, who was now making a show of wiping crumbs from the kitchen worktop. For heaven's sake, there were better things she could be doing with her afternoon than batting away minor affronts. Sister Irene could never let a meeting between them pass without getting some digs in. She could be rude in such polite ways that she sometimes left her unsuspecting targets emotionally bruised but bewildered as to exactly what had happened. Mark her words, Sister Veronica had witnessed it happening, and Sister Irene a woman of the cloth. She should be ashamed of herself.

'Oh, I don't think so, Sister. The peel always gets stuck in my teeth.' She glanced indiscreetly at the kitchen clock. 'Now if you'll excuse me, I'm off to the youth hostel.' Sister Veronica picked up her bag.

'Going to see that strange creature, Jamie, are you?' Sister Irene asked, her eyes widening a fraction.

'I'm sure I'll see young Jamie while I'm there, yes,' Sister Veronica replied. 'And I don't think he's strange, just a little damaged by something. You can see it in his eyes.' She wasn't going to let on that Jamie fascinated her. The way he seemed to live inside his head, his brooding countenance, his pained eyes. She'd taken to studying him carefully, and he was dangerously close to becoming a character in her book.

'Well you'd know, I'm sure.' Sister Irene's eyes flared. What on earth did she mean by that? 'Have a good afternoon, Sister. Happy baking.' A self-satisfied smile flickered across her lips.

At half past three on the dot, trying to evacuate cantankerous thoughts about Sister Irene, Sister Veronica walked out of the convent, pulling the front door shut behind her with a bang. Emerging from the stone porch and glancing left and right, she satisfied herself that Father Mathers was not about. The last thing she wanted to do was bump into him today. She was looking forward to her friend Father John's arrival at the hostel; he could always be counted on to knock at the door around half past four every weekday afternoon. Now at least with him there was a chance of sane conversation. And unlike Sister Irene, he didn't view poor Jamie as strange. If anything, he seemed rather protective over the boy. The students tended to arrive back in dribs and drabs soon after Father John's appearance, all hungry and all expecting cake. Sister Veronica enjoyed their vibrancy; their energy and carefree attitudes.

A yellowing atmosphere pervaded Soho Square Gardens. The people on the grass had lost the happy countenance of yesterday's sun-worshippers; today's seemed listless, all silently still as though in a tableau of depression.

Although she had a key to the hostel, she always felt it was polite to knock, just in case she took Jamie by surprise. He was such a fragile-looking thing she didn't want to startle him, and he seemed to have taken to her for some reason, always striking up stilted conversations.

Arriving outside the faded white door, she rapped loudly three times. The usual scurrying footsteps did not materialise. She tried again, then rummaged for the key.

The door clicked open. It was strangely quiet. Perhaps Jamie was having a lie down, or maybe he'd popped out to the shops. She hoped he had, it would do him good to get out more.

'Hello?' Sister Veronica called, heaving her bag of goods inside and shutting the door behind her. 'Jamie, are you there?'

No answer. Well, she'd make a start anyway.

As she unpacked the jar of jam, eggs, flour and butter onto the kitchen counter, a warm breeze wafted her long skirt to and fro. Perhaps Jamie had left the back door open. Silly boy. Maybe where he hailed from in Kent it was safe enough to leave doors open when no one was in, but in London's West End it certainly wasn't.

Wandering through to the utility room she saw that the back door was indeed wide open. Hmm. She'd have to have a word with him about that.

She stopped, as though electrocuted by shock.

Through the open door she could see a pair of feet lying very still. They had Jamie's trainers on.

She leaned forward to look.

Jamie Markham lay amid the builders' rubble in the backyard, a pool of redness oozing out around his head. Congealed blood covered his matted brown hair, and his skull was crushed at the side.

4
***

Sister Veronica staggered back in shock. Her stomach twisted, and for a moment she wondered whether she was going to vomit.

After minutes that could have been hours, she forced herself to come to her senses, un-rooting herself from the lino tiles.

Police. She must call the police. Everyone who came to stay in the hostel had mobile phones these days, so there was only an old broken payphone in the corner of the living room. She must go back to the convent.

RAT-A-TAT-TAT!

The door knocker hammered as she approached the door from the inside.

'Who is it?' she called. She didn't recognise her own voice, it was high, brittle.

'Father Mathers,' the voice on the other side snapped in reply. 'Do please hurry up and open the door, good Sister. It's starting to rain.'

'What?' Sister Veronica whispered. The world had turned surreal.

RAT-A-TAT-TAT- TAT-TAT.

'Open this door, please! We're getting soaked.' Father Mathers' shout swam with righteous petulance.

There's a chance this man can help, Sister Veronica told herself as she fumbled with the Chubb lock, her fingers as helpful as dead weights. It doesn't matter if you like him or not, he can help. He must be able to help.

A hand grabbed the door after she released the lock, pulling it wide open.

There in front of her stood Father Mathers, very damp, his face contorting from irritation to magnanimity. Next to him, smoothly-dressed in black with the white on his dog collar shining, was Cardinal Moore, also dripping, his eyes immediately penetrating into Sister Veronica's glazed ones. During previous rare meetings, she'd always been fascinated by how the Cardinal's hawk eyes contrasted with his otherwise innocent baby face. He had a powerful air about him, no doubt about that; something about his height gave him a commanding appearance. Control had never been a quality near the top of Sister Veronica's favourite character trait list. But there was no time to think of that now.

'Well, aren't you going to ask us in, Sister?' Father Mathers laughed, as though they'd arrived at a jolly birthday party and the door had been opened by a shy child. 'His Eminence and I were just chatting about how wonderful a cup of tea would taste. Could you possibly let us come in to dry off a bit, and perhaps, er, put the kettle on?'

'Your Eminence. Father Mathers,' Sister Veronica said, drawing herself up, shaking. Come on, Veronica, she told herself. Get a dashed grip.

'Come quickly. Something terrible has happened,' she said. No other words were possible.

Seconds later, they all stood in the back garden, staring at the broken body that used to house Jamie Markham.

Sister Veronica wondered at the heinous things some people were capable of. She'd seen dead bodies before, of course, the first two being her own mother and father. Well, the man who she called her father, who she'd learnt in the cruellest way that day when she was thirteen, wasn't biologically related to her at all. She'd sat with parishioners as they took their last breaths, sometimes she'd been the only person there to ease them into the next dimension of being. And there was a next dimension, she could feel it. Consciousness was not just chemicals that disappeared when the heart stopped beating, no matter what *New Scientist* articles claimed, and mark her words she'd read a few in the dentist's waiting room. It was all very well banging on about quarks and tetraquarks, and that nothing was there before the Big Bang, but if science was to be considered alongside the biblical explanations for existence, then what made these quarks? What allowed there to be nothing before there was something? The next experience of life may not be the patriarchal set-up purported by tradition, but it was there all right.

But why, why, why would anyone do this to Jamie? Why? She'd noticed the scars on his wrists before, although he'd taken pains to hide them. Knew he had a tortured past, that he must have tried to kill himself. She'd never asked him about it, presumed he'd tell her if he wanted to. But he hadn't killed himself. He'd survived and gone on, and now someone had taken that new effort at life away from him. Her eyes moistened but she didn't care. There was no shame at mourning this horror, this unnecessary extinction of young life. Why does suffering exist?

'Appalling,' Cardinal Moore said, his words cutting across her nightmarish reverie. Father Mathers, she saw, had frozen. 'This is utterly appalling.'

'Yes,' Sister Veronica agreed quietly. 'It is.'

'And on church-run property.' The Cardinal glared. Sister Veronica's eyes snapped round to laser into his.

'Pardon, Your Eminence? Surely the tragedy here is the loss of Jamie's life. I was just on the way to call the police when–'

'No. No police, Sister. Not yet. This is a church matter, and must be dealt with by canonical law first, the highest law, one that comes before and above civil law.'

Sister Veronica shook her head frantically.

'But–' she began.

'And yes, of course the tragedy here is the poor boy's loss of life. Of course it is, God rest his soul. If you want justice served here as much as I do, we must turn the matter over to God, surely you can see that? Sadly, murder comes under *graviora delicta*, the most serious of all sins investigated under canon law. The ultimate source of canon law is God, whose will is manifested through divine law. How can you and I argue against that? God is the highest authority there is, good Sister. I merely serve God's will, as do you. And with such a serious sin as this we must take care to follow the necessary actions.'

'But murder is not just a sin, Your Eminence, it's a crime!' Sister Veronica's voice rose. 'What about the body? Surely the police–'

'Am I not making myself clear, Sister?' Cardinal Moore spat, anger muddying his usual restraint. 'Do you seek to argue with God? You, who have vowed to be obedient to him? There is no room for false prophets in the Roman Catholic Church, the one true church founded by Jesus, God's son. If you want to help then pray for this boy, commend him to the Lord. God's laws, divine law and through him canon law, are the only ones acceptable to him. As a messenger of the Lord I can promise you this. Didn't Matthew say, "Beware of false prophets, which come to you in sheep's clothing"? I am sure you are not one of these, Sister. One who has promised to serve God but strays from him in times of great difficulty. Then your service to God and the church would be meaningless, wouldn't it? No, listen to me, Sister. This murder has taken place on church-run property. Those who investigate canon law will deal with the body, I will personally supervise the matter. Does anyone else know of this?'

'No, not as far as I'm aware. I came to bake the students' cake, and discovered Jamie's body not ten minutes ago.' Sister Veronica still shook, but now with a rage so pure she could hardly contain it.

'Thank you, Sister. I know I can rely on your absolute support and discretion in this matter. You need not say more about it just now, but in time I have no doubt that the assessors will need to speak with you, while they gather the acta, the documents that will become the basis of their investigation.' Cardinal Moore spoke calmly now, but he moved closer. He's like a bird of prey bearing down on me, Sister Veronica thought. 'I am responsible here, don't forget,' the Cardinal continued, now very close to her. 'I have overseen many other cases within the jurisdiction of canonical law and I will see that God's will is done here, with yours and Father Mathers' help, of course.'

Turning abruptly, he addressed the priest, who'd unfrozen and had been following the exchange of words keenly.

'Father Mathers, see that this matter is kept private at all costs. The students and anyone else wanting to enter the hostel must be kept away.'

'Of course, Your Grace,' Father Mathers replied. 'You have my unending support; I will do everything I can to help you fulfil God's will in this and every matter. Where should the students go? All their belongings are in their rooms?'

'Find a solution. Do it discreetly and do not give a hint of any scandal. If journalists get hold of this story they will descend on us like rabid hyenas. Then all the good people of the cloth will yet again be attacked by inaccurate, deceiving, poisonous words.

We are taught in seminary, are we not, Father Mathers, of the importance of close brotherhood, enacted for us through the apostolic tradition? Well now is the time for that brotherhood – and, of course, sisterhood – to come together. We must close ranks, and do justice for the boy. We must protect Mother Church, and we must bring whoever committed this monstrous sin to justice, in the most unobtrusive way possible. In time we will have the *res iudicata*, the final conclusion to this case. Until then, let us pray for the boy and his family, and for guidance, and let us all act in a unified manner according to God's will.'

'Of course, Your Eminence. Sister Veronica and I will see this is done,' Father Mathers said, his eyes flashing towards the nun for a second. A warning shot?

'Good. I must go now, there is much I have to organise with this. And to think we came here to speak of press coverage. So much can change within twenty minutes. I will take my leave of you good people. God Bless you both.'

He turned and strode through the doorway back into the hostel, Father Mathers following like a lapdog.

Sister Veronica stared down at Jamie's body. I never promised anything, she thought. I was told what to do, but I never promised. My God would want me to help this boy, and that's what I'm going to do.

5

Ascending the hostel stairs as quietly as she could manage, Sister Veronica heard the low, murmured voices of Cardinal Moore and Father Mathers near the front door. Let them talk, she said to herself. Let the Cardinal warn Father Mathers to keep an eye on me, to make sure I behave. Knowing the clerics could not see the stairs from the front door, she trod on each stair as lightly as possible, her knees aching with the effort, willing each not to creak. She was glad they were talking. A few minutes' grace would serve her nicely.

Through the window on the first-floor landing, she caught a glimpse of a batch of bedraggled tourists faithfully following a tour guide down the street. The patch of wet grass at the centre of Soho Square was now empty, bar one dog walker. Strange how normal life goes on amid one's spiralling chaos, she thought. That must be what enables us to all keep going. Those in destruction and those in normality are carried along together, offset by each other, stuck together in this peculiar jigsaw we call life.

Now, which of these rooms was Jamie's? She'd kept to the ground floor before, never finding it necessary to impose on the personal spaces of hostel-stayers, unless one had left and the room needed cleaning.

The first door she opened let out a pungent perfumed smell. Bottles of hair and beauty products were scattered across the desk, and the duvet was a soft pink colour, a French novel thrown on top of it. Probably that pretty girl Celine's room. She closed the door and tried more, but none of them seemed like Jamie's. He was fastidiously neat, she'd noticed, to a point of obsession, and none of the rooms had that feel about them. However, opening the second-to-last door along the corridor, and seeing the bare-looking room, with its black duvet stretched meticulously over the bed, the three biros lined up with precision on the desk, and no other objects in sight anywhere else, suggested she may have found what she was looking for.

Entering the room, she imagined Jamie with her, staring at her in the intense way he'd had. Who were you? she asked him. What can you tell me that will let me help you?

Practical enough to feel no sense of guilt at going through a deceased person's belongings, Sister Veronica began searching the room. Opening the wardrobe doors exposed a rail of neatly-hung shirts, mainly jeans and hooded tops, each hanger spaced evenly apart. She fingered through them, patting the pockets of the hoodies. The bottom of the cupboard was bare, apart from an empty sports bag. She drew back the plain blue curtains and looked behind. Only a spider. Going over to the desk, she pulled open the top drawer, revealing neatly-rolled socks and underwear. The one beneath contained T-shirts folded and stacked to a mathematical degree, and the one beneath that, a vast selection of pills, as well as bottles of deodorant and shampoo. Sister Veronica picked up one of the pill packets and read, *Sertraline 200mg*. What was that? Another said *Lithium Carbonate 1.5g*. Puzzled by the extent of the boy's pharmaceutical stockpile, she closed the drawer and gazed at the biros on the desk. Now, if you have biros, you must have been writing something. But what?

Glancing round the room told her that the only other visible items were a pair of worn-looking black shoes. With great effort and wincing at the effect on her knees, she slowly crouched down and peered under the bed. Nothing. She lifted up the mattress, unsettling the perfectly folded sheet. Well, it wouldn't matter now. Jamie was somewhere else, and she prayed he was at peace. Nothing there either.

What an empty room. It was sad, she felt, that this amounted to the existence of the boy. No pictures or photos on the wall, no books or signs of any hobby. Where was his art? Wasn't he supposed to be an art student? She felt an uneasiness. Who on earth had Jamie Markham really been? She needed to approach the room differently. She hadn't been through enough. With renewed rigour she took initiative and reopened the middle drawer of the desk, lifting up the pile of T-shirts, revealing a dog-eared plain black diary. Seizing it, she flicked through the pages. Where was April? Ah yes. She flicked to the date, and stared. The only entry for that day said *Today's the day: Tell Sister Veronica*. Jamie had drawn a smiley face in a perfect circle next to the words. Tell Sister Veronica what?

Footsteps on the stairs made her instinctively shove the diary under the duvet. She opened the wardrobe door and seized a handful of shirts, hangers slipping as she dragged them out.

'Sister Veronica! What on earth are you doing?' Father Mathers stood in the doorway, aghast.

'I'm following His Eminence's instructions, Father Mathers. The Cardinal clearly said that no students must be allowed back, so obviously they need to be housed elsewhere. If they can't be here, then we need to quickly clear their belongings out, don't we? This room looked like it needed the least work, so I thought I'd start here. I'm quite surprised it's taken you this long to come and help, given the gravity of the situation. Not only do we need to do this, but we need to find somewhere else for the students to stay.' She looked him squarely in the eye.

'Heaven's above, you wretched woman. What if this is Jamie's room? The assessors won't want his possessions touched. That is the first thing we need to establish, which room was the boy's, and leave it just so. Honestly, no logic.' Father Mathers' shock must have completely left him as his pomposity was in full force. 'I'll start at one end of the corridor and make my way up, you start at this end and we will establish which room is his; look for identifiable features, name tags, anything.' He went off. Sister Veronica grabbed the diary, it fitted into the deep pocket of her skirt. She hung the shirts back up, nowhere as neatly as Jamie had done, then went out of the room and opened the end door very loudly, making a great show.

Before long, Father Mathers had established that the room the nun had been messing about in was indeed Jamie's and he shook his head like a disappointed schoolteacher.

'Have you replaced the shirts, Sister? Exactly as you found them? Good. Then I think we don't need to mention your faux pas to anyone. His Eminence is distraught enough as it is, and we don't want to make matters even worse. But learn from this and be more restrained in all other actions, please. Now let's get on with emptying the other rooms.'

They were down to the last two rooms, packing the contents in large black bin bags Sister Veronica had found under the sink, when she heard cheery voices from outside, and a key turning in the lock.

'The students are back,' Father Mathers called imperiously from the next-door room. 'I'll go down and explain something to them while you finish the rooms. Can't have you messing anything else up today, can we, Sister?'

She heard him go down the stairs and intercept the students at the door.

'We're terribly sorry,' she could hear him explaining, 'but unfortunately a severe carbon monoxide leak has been identified and the building has been deemed unsafe to live in for now. Yes, yes, Sister Veronica is packing up your belongings at the moment, but the authorities have told us that none of you are to be allowed back in, for your own safety. We are awfully sorry for the inconvenience, please accept this money and go to the café down the street. We are in the process of finding you alternative accommodation. Yes, it will be free of charge, as you've already paid your hostel fees. One of us will come and get you when we know where that is.'

'How easily lying comes to you, Father Mathers,' Sister Veronica said under her breath, as she tied a knot in a bulging bag. 'Almost as though you're practised at it.' She was certain Cardinal Moore would be thoroughly overjoyed at being billed for accommodation for the students, but this secrecy was at his insisting, so he would dashed well pay for the blasted collateral damage.

A new voice from outside made her stop her work and pause.

'What's going on here?' It was Father John's voice. 'Is everything all right?'

Father Mathers lowered his voice so she couldn't hear his reply, but she was certain he wouldn't be divulging the truth. Oh no, he had his eye on bigger things in life, just as she was sure Cardinal Moore had his eye on Rome. Neither of them would compromise their ambitions, she would bet her entire stash of writings on it.

'We'll call you later then, Father John,' Father Mathers said loudly, a few minutes later. 'Let you know how the students are. Yes, yes, she's fine, please don't worry.'

Well that's a pity. Sister Veronica sighed. She had an insatiable desire to talk to a friend, to someone who cared more about others than their own reputation and desires. Of course, she couldn't tell them about the terrible things that had occurred today, but having contact with human compassion when times were tough was healing almost above all else, in her opinion. By Jove, she didn't know how she was going to handle this. Not just Jamie's murder, but the Cardinal's reaction to it. Surely it wasn't right? Surely the police needed to know?

Later that evening, after the students had been split up and rehoused in three other hostels across London, the chaos of their belongings in bin bags had finally been sorted out and returned to the rightful owners. Cardinal Moore was fully updated, and the carbon monoxide cover story spread liberally throughout the convent. The keys of the next-door hostel had been handed over to two men dressed all in black, with no dog collars, who strode up to the convent at twenty to six in the evening bringing a decidedly chilly air with them – presumably the Cardinal's assessors although Sister Veronica couldn't possibly say as they'd hardly introduced themselves.

She'd finally had a chance to sit down with a cup of tea and some toast. She'd brought them up to her room, not caring if this would be frowned on by Sister Irene. Starving, emotionally battered, angry, perplexed and overwhelmingly exhausted, all she wanted was to eat and drink, then lie down and have a proper read of Jamie's diary and try to find out what on earth he meant by *Tell Sister Veronica*.

There was a gentle tap-tap-tap at her door.

'What?' she roared, slamming the plate of toast onto her desk. 'What is it?' If it was Sister Irene, with a basket of apples and a homily about toast crumbs, she could–

'Only me,' Sister Agnes' gentle voice called. 'It doesn't sound like a good time, Veronica, should I come back tomorrow?'

'No.' Sister Veronica heaved herself up and opened the door. 'No, sorry, Agnes, come in. I've had such a day. I'm glad you're here actually, I need to ask you something.'

She stood aside so that her friend, stooping slightly, could shuffle in. Her eyes glanced down at Sister Agnes' swollen, red knuckles, and her knobbly, misshapen fingers that stuck out randomly like branches on an old tree.

'How's the pain?' she asked, supporting her friend's elbows as she lowered herself slowly onto the edge of Sister Veronica's bed.

'Oh you know, comes and goes.' Sister Agnes had no time for self-indulgence, especially when it came to illness. Sister Veronica always remembered the time when Sister Agnes had told her about a particular incident from her childhood. Her parents had kept horses, who she claimed her mother had doted on much more than her five children. One day, Agnes, her mother, and two of her brothers had been off on a hack, cantering over open fields near their house, when Agnes' horse had been startled by a tractor suddenly swinging into the field. It became skittish, jumping sideways, and Agnes fell off, landing hard on her backside and fracturing her coccyx. Her mother's only advice, seeing her daughter writhe in agony in the subsequent days, was to tell her to rub the affected area hard with a brick. Sister Veronica suspected that this played a key part in Sister Agnes' continuing dismissal of her own and anyone else's pain, but still, it affected her to see her friend's laboured movements and inflamed joints.

Sister Veronica saw her friend eyeing her carefully.

'Have you got any more writing for me to read yet?' Sister Agnes asked, resting her hands on her lap. 'I could do with a distraction from this infernal heat.'

'Nothing worth showing you, I'm afraid.' Sister Veronica turned her desk chair around and sat down. She attempted to slow her breaths, she needed to decelerate her panicking heart rate and for the revulsion in her head to subside. She didn't want to lie to her friend, but what choice did she have? 'This week's been unusually busy, what with the girl Melissa's interview, and packing up the students' belongings today. I smelt like a perfume factory after bundling up Celine's room.'

'Hmm. Strange business, this carbon monoxide leak.' Sister Agnes' beady eyes glinted. While her body had its pains, her mind was the sharpest in the convent, in Sister Veronica's opinion, it didn't miss a trick. She badly wanted to tell her friend exactly what had happened today but she daren't. The horror, coursing through her veins the minute she'd found Jamie, had multiplied and gone off on tangents after the Cardinal's reaction. She'd felt the heavy weight of danger descend on her when the police were not allowed to be called, so apart from anything else she didn't want to involve her already vulnerable friend in this murkiness. But oh how she longed to confide in Agnes. 'Especially after the health and safety chap signed the hostel devices off as safe not more than a month ago. Sister Irene was beside herself with the fact we didn't need to spend any money buying new ones.'

Sister Veronica's smile was ghostly-weak.

'All I can say is that's what the students were told,' she said. 'And another thing I can say, Agnes, is that I need to ask your advice about something. Now, this is going to sound strange but I'm going to have to ask you to trust me, and not to ask me any details, because I simply can't say at the moment. I have no doubt it will all come out in the end, but for now please don't press me on this.' She looked at her friend, who stared back, then nodded. 'You and your clever mind have been following the reports into the clerical sexual abuse disgraces, haven't you? I know you've been interested in the legalities.'

'I've certainly read about them in the papers,' Sister Agnes replied. One aspect connected to her rheumatism that she didn't object to, was being allowed to read and rest in the library down the road several times a week. Her gnarled hands made it impossible for her to help with most of the nuns' chores like cooking, cleaning and gardening, so a few years ago Mother Superior had suggested Sister Agnes might like to try the library as a diversion to keep her occupied, a proposition that had been readily agreed with. 'It's all smoke and mirrors.' The two nuns had established a long time ago that they both felt out of sorts with the management and power within the Catholic Church. It wasn't something they spoke of often, one had to be so careful, but it was comforting to know a shared view existed.

'All right, so tell me this. Is canonical law really put above civil law in cases where sins or crimes have been committed within the church's remit?'

Sister Agnes raised her eyebrows.

'Yes,' she said. 'This has happened in many cases. In 2009, the Murphy Report showed that in Ireland, bishops and archbishops had been supplied with multiple batches of conclusive evidence about priests who'd abused children, but dealt with this internally and never told the police. When the judge questioned them about this in court, they defended their decisions, despite suicides of the young victims in question being brought to the fore. They talked about how in civil law, defamation can only be committed through untruthful statements, but how in church law defamation encompasses both the sin of calumny *and* the sin of detraction. Detraction is the undue destroying of another's good name by the exposure of some mistake or lawbreaking of which the person is in fact responsible, or at any rate is seriously believed to be guilty of by the accuser.'

Sister Veronica's stomach heaved.

'Do you mean,' she said, 'that under church law, even if

someone is guilty, it is against the law to accuse them as guilty of the sin or crime committed, because you would be damaging their reputation?'

'Yes, that's exactly what I'm saying,' Sister Agnes replied. 'Evidence in the Murphy Report states it clearly. I remember it so well because it repelled me to read it.'

Sister Veronica banged her fist down hard on her desk. Tears flowed from her eyes.

'What exactly is this institution we're part of, Agnes?' she asked, her mind a pool of darkness. 'This duplicity and dishonesty makes me sick to my soul. It makes a mockery of St Paul's belief in love as greater than all things. I'm no fool, I've been aware of the more corrupt sides of the church for some time now. I mean, how can one not be? But this? This is too much. I can no longer be involved with the tenets of this organisation. Where is God in the church nowadays? Why have men's egos overtaken basic truth? And love? Clearly no longer necessary. Oh, the hypocrisy.' Her fist thumped down on the desk again. She experienced a deep shudder of knowing as the sheer enormity of the murder, the secrecy, her involvement, and Cardinal Moore's immediate instinct to put the welfare of the church's reputation over and above justice for Jamie sunk in.

Sister Agnes let her friend's sobs subside until they sat quietly together, solitude calming the pain. Then she leaned forward.

'Now, listen here, Veronica. No, look at me, and listen to what I've got to say. I don't know what went on in the hostel today, and I'm not going to ask. But what I do know is that you shouldn't give up, not now. Don't you dare. My body's too broken for me to be of any use, but you still have your health, and you have the passion to bring some light into whatever darkness you're seeing. I agree with you, there's a stench of corruption that runs deeply in this institution, and I hate it. Oh, there's plenty of good

SARAH SHERIDAN

people, but so many are being misled by those drunk with power. I can't do anything about it, but you can. We've made our beds here, but we don't have to lie in them. Can't you see that? You can do something, anything that will help. Whatever it is that's happened, if it's being covered up, you don't have to be one of those who sits mildly by and does nothing. I don't think you would ever do that anyway,' Sister Agnes finished with a wry smile. 'You're too bloody-minded.'

Sister Veronica gazed at her friend. She breathed several times very deeply. She thought about Jamie's words, how he was going to tell her something. Was it more than a coincidence that he was murdered on the same day that he planned to reveal information to her? Damn it all. A small part of her wanted to ignore all this, until it went away. But a larger, lioness part of her reared up in anger and protection towards Jamie.

'Looks like I won't have much time for writing in the near future then, doesn't it?' she said.

Opening her bedroom door to see her friend off, the sight of the fire door at the end of the corridor closing made her start. Had someone been listening to their conversation? No, stop it, Veronica. It's probably one of the sisters going off to have a bath. She would not give in to the clawing hands of paranoia, no matter how hard they tried to get her in their grasp. Another much worse realisation entered her mind. She was dealing with an appalling murder here. There was a killer on the loose, possibly in the convent itself. What if that person had overheard everything? If they had, would her own life now be under threat?

6

Melissa Carlton lay on her narrow bed, strands of golden and pink hair splayed across the pillow. A new nicotine patch slapped on the inside of her arm, she breathed out with relief as the irritation induced by withdrawal receded. She had vague plans to give up smoking, but that certainly wasn't top of her priority list right now. Bloody hell, she couldn't keep this up for long, or she'd be a wreck. She was wondering what the actual fuck had happened to her life. One minute she'd been a party-loving, hard-working, hard-living journalist, the next minute she was holed up in a convent without her phone, on an insane one-person mission that at best felt surreal, and at worst, rash, badly-planned and disastrous. And all for this bloody secret that had been shoved on her, that she didn't want.

She didn't believe in fate but some events were too synchronistic to go unnoticed. The internal workings of this convent were complex, it didn't take a genius to see that. On the surface, the sisters, and the priests when they came, had given up their free will, and their official line was that they all had callings to serve God. As far as she could tell, Sister Irene was the only old girl who believed what she said one hundred per cent. But things were not as straightforward as they seemed. Some people's individuality wasn't squashed yet; in particular, Sister Veronica's eyes spoke louder than words.

When the co-ordinator of the secret French support group, the one that helped all the other people round the world who'd been born into the same secret unwanted club she'd been, had given her the name Jamie Markham: 'He's in Westminster too, try and find him', it hadn't taken her long to find out that he worked in the hostel next door. She blinked with frustration. Why had she left it so long to talk to him? What if it was too late now? From what she'd seen and heard over the last day she wondered if she'd ever get a chance now. For God's sake, she was an idiot to get into all this in the first place.

Her mission – for what? Answers? Recognition? Peace? – had taken an unexpected turn yesterday. It was beyond strange and worrying. What she'd witnessed outside the hostel, after asking Mother Superior if she could pop to the chemist on the pretext of getting necessary 'ladies' products', kept playing in her mind. She recalled the scene intensely, raking it over, trying to make sense of the details. How come she'd left the convent, desperate for some new nicotine patches, and been present at the exact moment it happened? There was one woman who could help her, but she felt with all her intuition that she was the last person Sister Veronica would want to talk to at the moment. But there was no way in hell she was going to give up, she was just going to have to make the old nun listen. Of course, she'd have to confess to her that she hadn't just come to the convent to investigate and write a piece on 'How Nuns Live', although she was doing that too, her editor had loved the idea when she'd pitched it. Her journalistic purpose justified her presence, and diverted attention away from her real motive. No one had looked at her strangely so far, apart from Sister Veronica. And she looked at everyone like they were half-baked. She'd almost given herself away when she'd interviewed the old girl in the garden; let her guard down for a moment, and Sister Veronica had clocked that something was up. But there was no way she could have known what it was. She hoped she'd be able to win Sister Veronica's confidence, but she had a hit-and-miss history with that kind of thing. How had Darren, her dickhead ex, ceremoniously dumped last Friday, described her? 'You're fucking crazy,' he'd hissed as she'd walked away from him. 'And your heart is stone. You're going to die lonely, and that's just what you deserve.' This wasn't true, her heart was most definitely not made from stone. In truth, she'd always had too many emotions to deal with but she found a hard shell a good defence against the world, and Darren. He'd changed from attentive to critical over the two years they'd spent together, so there'd been no other option, he'd had to go. One thing Melissa was good at doing was walking away from a problem. Would she walk away from this too?

She already knew the answer. No, she wouldn't – couldn't – walk away from this one. She was no shrink, but she did sometimes worry that she was crazy, she had such a fluid sense of identity, she didn't feel like she knew who she was at all, and she highly suspected this was because of her parental situation; biological and adoptive. It was so bloody clichéd it was unbelievable. Her anxiety, that she usually managed to hide in the daytime, had been in overdrive at night; racing thoughts, a floating sense of being outside her body, it all felt out of control. It was scary and she wanted it to stop. She looked younger than her twenty-nine years – everybody said so. But inside her the ubiquitous clock was ticking, and she wanted to meet someone, maybe even have a kid, before she was in danger of becoming one of those mums in the playground that everyone thought was a granny. But that wasn't likely to happen until she got to the root of the problem. She was doing this for herself, Melissa knew. She was finally going to sort herself out.

Minutes later, nicotine patch hidden under a long, flowing shirt, she rapped at Sister Veronica's door. A low grumbling could be heard, then the door opened.

'I hope I'm not disturbing you?' Melissa smiled brightly.

The look of sheer resignation and dismay on the nun's face answered her question.

'I'm sorry, Melissa, but I'm a bit busy at the moment,' Sister Veronica said gruffly, closing the door. Melissa's foot arrived swiftly as a doorstop.

'With respect, Sister Veronica,' Melissa said, her voice lower. 'I need to talk to you. Sorry to sound dramatic, but I'm not leaving your room until I have.'

'Melissa!' The nun was instantly angry. 'Have you forgotten yourself?'

Melissa sighed. She was going to have to bring the big guns out.

'It's about Jamie Markham,' she whispered.

Sister Veronica's eyes snapped in to focus.

'You'd better come in,' she said.

The nun's bedroom wasn't the sparse space Melissa had been expecting. It was a place of business; a wodge of papers and notebooks was piled high on the desk with an old black notebook on top, pens strewn around, an empty plate at one end. The bed was roughly made, the crumpled duvet suggested Sister Veronica had been lying on top of it recently. A skirt was thrown over the back of the desk chair, and a stash of books piled up in one corner of the room.

Sister Veronica turned the desk chair around roughly, motioned for Melissa to sit down, then sat on the bed.

'Well?' she said.

'Look, I don't really know where to start.' Melissa glanced at the door, checking it was shut. 'I haven't been completely honest with you, Sister. I'm here for more reasons than just research.'

Sister Veronica waited, wondering what on earth the girl was going to say.

Melissa took a deep breath.

'I've known for three years now that my birth mother is a nun. I was brought up knowing I was adopted, but with no information about who my biological parents were. On her deathbed, my aunt told me the truth, she said I had a right to know. She said my birth mother was a nun from the Diocese of Westminster, but that my adoptive parents didn't want me to know. They are very Catholic, they want to protect the church. My mum was furious with my aunt, she won't tell me my birth mother's name, and my aunt didn't know. There's a support group for the children of clergy in France, I found it on the internet. I started googling biological children of nuns the minute I found out, I wanted to speak to someone in the same situation, I felt so isolated, you can't imagine. Then one day this group popped up. I got in touch with them, and they've really helped me. They put me in touch with other nuns' and priests' children, it turns out there's loads of us, but we've all been kept secret. When I told the guy from the support group that I was a journalist, he suggested I find a way to gain access to the Diocese of Westminster, he says you get so much more knowledge when you work with the Catholic Church rather than against it. I'd tried everything else to find my birth mother and failed, so I thought I'd give it a go. I didn't mean any harm, Sister, honestly. I just want to find my biological mother so badly. You don't know what it's like, not knowing who your real parents are.'

The old nun continued staring at her, unblinking.

'Just before I arrived at the Convent of the Christian Heart, the group's co-ordinator sent me a message. He said he'd heard another child of clergy was about in Westminster, the child of a priest, called Jamie Markham. He said I should try and find him, and that maybe we could help each other.'

With this information, Sister Veronica's eyes filled with pain and tears, and she sagged as though hit by an unseen weapon, but still she sat, staring at Melissa.

'A couple of days ago, I found out that Jamie worked at the hostel next door. I overheard Sister Irene telling Sister Maria what an untalkative boy he was. I was planning to go and speak to him, but I wanted to interview the sisters first. I didn't know how Jamie would react when I spoke to him, and if he blew my cover I wouldn't be able to stay here anymore.' Melissa sighed. 'Then yesterday, after I asked Mother Superior if I could pop to the shops to get something I badly needed, I saw some men dressed in black going into the youth hostel. It was after the whole drama with the carbon monoxide leak. They didn't look like technicians, one had a gold cross round his neck. The other was wheeling a big suitcase through the hostel door. It just seemed really strange.'

The pain and hurt in Sister Veronica's eyes intensified.

'I really regretted not talking to Jamie while I had the chance, and now that the students have been rehoused all over London I thought I better get in touch with him before I lost the opportunity forever. So this morning I told Sister Julia I had a meeting I'd forgotten about with my editor, and that I really must go to it. She wasn't pleased, but she agreed. I know this was a little bit of an untruth, Sister, but I really had to find Jamie.'

Sister Veronica responded to this information with an unflinching agony-filled gaze.

'So then,' Melissa said, 'I went to all the hostels Sister Catherine said the students had been rehomed in, looking for him. But he wasn't in any of them, and the students said they hadn't seen him since yesterday morning at breakfast. One of them gave me his mobile number, and I tried to ring it from a payphone – Mother Superior said she wouldn't give me my phone back till the end of the week – but it just went to voicemail. I know this sounds strange, Sister, but I'm really worried about him. Do you know where he is?'

Sister Veronica considered this question.

7

'It seems to me,' she said heavily, 'that so much has been going on right under my nose, and that I've missed it all.'

Sister Veronica's head was reeling. Jamie, the child of a priest? Was that what he was going to tell her yesterday? Was this why someone had killed him, to silence him?

The parallels between Jamie and Melissa's stories and her own life were too excruciating to contemplate, yet they couldn't be ignored. And she had thought she was the only one. She'd found out that day, when she was thirteen, when she'd gone into the church with a message from her mum for the priest about the flowers. A reptilian chill permeated her skin as she remembered how she'd gone into the church, calling Father Dominic's name, eventually finding the priest in the vestry.

He'd been hoping she'd pop in, he said. Her mother had said she might. Yes, yes, a new flower arrangement on Saturday afternoon would be just the thing. She hadn't immediately understood the predatory hunger in the priest's eyes. But when he'd pushed her against the wall and done unspeakable things to her, she'd understood. 'Bad girl,' he'd said. 'You've made me do this. Look at the dress you wore. This is our little secret.' Even now, as the flashback tormented her, she could smell that awful mustiness laced with incense and candle wax, feel his body against hers. Afterwards, with hot tears falling down her cheeks formed from terror and disgust, she'd whispered:

'You're a bad man. I'm going to tell my father.'

'Your father?' The priest had laughed. 'You silly girl, has no one told you? He's no father of yours. You are just like your mother now, a dirty whore. No one will believe you, least of all that poor cuckolded man. Your real father's been moved on now. Why do you think Father Simon left the parish all those years ago?'

Weeks later, when she could speak again, she'd asked her mother.

'Was my real daddy Father Simon?'

Her mother had wept. 'Shhh,' she'd said. 'Who told you? Don't ever mention this again. I was wrong, Veronica, I did a bad thing. But I atone for my sins every day. We must protect the church's good name, Veronica. Don't mention this, even to your father. It hurts him too much. Just forget you ever found out, put it out of your mind, do you hear? I never want to hear another word about this.'

But things had never been the same again. She – Veronica – had atoned too, every day, for her parents' sins, for the priest's sin, and for her sin. Until one day, as she stood on top of a waterfall near their farm, looking down, down, down at the water crashing on the rocks below. I could be crashing on the rocks too – the thought sped through her mind in a second. And the pain would be over. Then she realised. This is their guilt. I can't carry it anymore. In a split second she'd felt free. Not completely free, just as though a certain weight had disappeared. What had remained was an incandescent anger, a seething spark of rage at the baseless lack of humanity in some people that caused them to hurt others. And when that lack of humanity came from people of the cloth, priests and nuns, her rage became unending. With the new knowledge Melissa had brought today, Jamie's fight had instantly become her own. Their suffering was the same, but Jamie was dead, killed – it seemed – to cover another's mistake.

Now, she regarded the girl in front of her. If everything Melissa said could be trusted, there was a very real chance that the girl could now also be in danger. Her instinct told her that Melissa was telling the truth. Oh, how she wished none of this had happened, how she longed for her previous life of just two days ago. But it *had* happened, and for some reason God and the universe had chosen to make her a key cog in its wheel. A strange calmness came over her. She would do what needed to be done, no matter what the consequences. And God protect anyone who got in her way. She frowned.

'Melissa,' she said slowly, 'I am about to tell you something that you must promise not to tell anyone, ANYONE, for your own sake.'

The girl nodded.

'Jamie is dead. And from what you've told me, I have reason to believe your life might be in danger too.'

'What do you mean, dead?' Shock rendered Melissa's face ghostly white. 'How do you know?'

Sister Veronica got up, opened her bedroom door, and looked both ways down the corridor. Then she closed the door, sat back down on her bed, and told Melissa about yesterday's events. About going over to the hostel with the ingredients, finding Jamie's body, the visit from the Cardinal and Father Mathers, and Cardinal Moore's decision to keep the matter within canonical law.

'But he can't do that.' Melissa's protest was loud. 'It's illegal. What about Jamie's parents and family?'

'They'll be paid off, I expect,' Sister Veronica said darkly. 'Hush money, whether they want it or not. Sometimes confidentiality agreements are forced on people, and they're legally binding. I went to the library early this morning to read how church law has handled clerical sexual abuse cases, I wanted to understand the precedents for Cardinal Moore's actions. Often large sums of money have been swapped for the family's silence, and I'll bet that's what will happen here.'

Melissa's body folded until it was bent double in the chair, her hands took hold of large clumps of her hair and gripped until her knuckles became taut and white. When her sobs started, they were violent and noisy, a primal reaction to a universal horror. Sister Veronica stood up and placed her hand on Melissa's back, waiting for the inevitable onslaught to pass.

While she waited, a series of questions pressed forward in her mind and clamoured for attention. Why had Jamie been killed? And more to the point, who on earth had killed him? Was it an inside job or a burglary gone wrong? The thought that the killer could still be roaming the convent was ghastly, but one that must be faced nevertheless. Perhaps Jamie had been involved with the wrong sort of people; he had enough pills to open a pharmacy. Who was Jamie's father? Was the father involved, was he killed to stop Jamie telling anyone of his connection with the ordained? Something that had been troubling her since yesterday pressed forward too. Was the Cardinal really within his rights not to report this matter to the police?

Saints alive, how on earth was she going to set about answering even one of these questions? Reading Jamie's diary last night hadn't told her much, the entries were very short and perfunctory: *Arrived in Soho, Talked to Dominique, Spoke to Victor, have agreed to do it.* Who were Dominique and Victor? Certainly none of the hostel students went by those names. What had he agreed to do? The questions were mounting but so far she could answer none of them.

Thoughts of her murder-mystery manuscript flashed through her mind. In the seven crime stories she'd completed so far, she always made her detective character, DI Nancarrow, follow a process when he investigated murders. He assessed the crime scene, spoke to witnesses, collected evidence and interviewed suspects. She made sure he wrote down everything, creating a timeline of events, and he had to follow every lead. He looked for what instigated the murder, the motivation behind it, and most importantly, who the killer could be. Fine, this was fiction and what she was dealing with was real life. But it was all the structure she had, so it just might help. She'd have to go back to the hostel and take another look, for starters. See if there were any clues that pointed to who committed this heinous crime.

After several minutes, the girl's sobs quietened and her breathing levelled.

'This is too horrible.' Melissa's voice was muffled. 'I can't believe this is happening. I can't handle this. If I'd gone to talk to Jamie earlier, maybe I could have helped him. Maybe this wouldn't have happened.'

'Maybe it would, maybe it wouldn't.' Sister Veronica felt ruthless, but she had to get through to the girl. 'Maybe if I'd gone over earlier, or taken more time to get to know the boy, it wouldn't have happened either. But neither of us killed Jamie. That was someone else, maybe more than one person. The guilt lies with them, not us, and it won't bring him back to torment ourselves with blame.'

Melissa managed a watery smile.

'You're as sharp as a knife, aren't you, Sister? I thought you were different from the rest of them.'

'Oh, and why's that?' Sister Veronica couldn't help herself.

'It's the way you look at people, like you're constantly observing. Your eyes seem to take in everything.'

It was Sister Veronica's turn to manage a watery smile.

'I do love people-watching,' she said. 'I always have. It's how I make sense of the world. Right. What we need,' she said, getting up and bustling about, 'is a bit of normality for a minute or two. And there's nothing more normal than a packet of custard cream biscuits.'

A few minutes later, they both sat with a pile of biscuits in their hands, Melissa nibbling hers and Sister Veronica working quickly through her batch with remarkable application.

'I never really liked these,' Melissa said. 'But at the moment they don't taste too bad.'

'Best thing ever invented, in my opinion,' Sister Veronica said stoutly, reaching again for the packet.

The peak of the shockwave had broken, and the crisis – while still in full swing – was at least laid out bare for them both to see. Melissa rubbed the side of her head.

'Hang on,' she turned to the nun. 'What did you mean when you said you think my life might be in danger too?'

'My dear.' Sister Veronica shook her head. 'There's more I need to tell you. Yesterday, as the Cardinal was leaving, I went upstairs to look in Jamie's room. I feel as strongly as you do that the powers that be are not handling this case in an ethical or moral way. They are protecting themselves, their reputations, and the public image of the church. They don't seem to care about getting justice for Jamie, they just want it all cleaned up as quickly and as quietly as possible. You said before that I couldn't know what it's like to not know your parentage, or the desire to find your roots. I'm afraid you're wrong there, Melissa, I know that feeling very well. This seems an unbelievable thing for me to admit to you, because no one else in this convent knows, but when I was thirteen, I was told that my real father was the local priest, Father Simon. He was transferred to another parish soon after my mother gave birth, and the matter was never spoken of again. I always thought I was the only priest's child in existence until you told me about yourself and Jamie, and this group. I am now no longer alone in this, it's a wonderful and terrifying feeling. Although I'm finding it hard to comprehend the numbers of priests' and nuns' children in existence that you seem to be implying.'

'I know, I know exactly how you feel,' Melissa said. 'I couldn't believe it either. But you have to believe me, Sister Veronica. I can show you the group, I can introduce you to some of the others. There are loads of us. Honestly, it's the best kept secret since they discovered the world was round.' Melissa's eyes bored into hers imploringly. 'If you think about it, it kind of makes sense. Priests and nuns are human too. Taking a vow of celibacy one day might seem a good idea, but forever is a long time. This was going to be the subject of my next article, after the one about this convent. I've already started making notes for it. Cardinal Wolsey, in Henry VIII's time, confessed to having at least two kids. Erasmus was the son of a Catholic priest. You can see on Wikipedia that lots of popes have admitted to fathering loads of kids. We've always been out there, we've just never known about each other before. The internet is a wonderful thing.'

'It sometimes is, it sometimes isn't, from what I hear,' Sister Veronica said. 'I've never really used it. Technology tends to give me a headache.'

They sat quietly for a minute.

'It might be safer for you to return home, Melissa,' Sister Veronica said gently. Seeing the girl distraught, and learning of their shared experiences had softened her feelings considerably. 'We could make up a story, say you're feeling sick and need to go?'

Melissa grimaced.

'Go where? Home to my empty apartment, knowing everything that I do, and just resume normal life as though I don't have a care in the bloody world? Yeah, that's such a realistic option.' Her face dropped into a cold, detached look and she turned away.

'I can't allow anything else to happen here, not now I know all that I do. I'm trying to think about your safety, Melissa, can't you see that?' It came out more sharply than Sister Veronica had intended. 'A boy has been killed, do you understand? This is a dangerous place, and while you're here, you could be a sitting target. And I will not allow that, not on my watch. The best thing is for you to return home immediately.' She lowered her eyes. 'If I'm quite honest, I need to think about how best to protect my own safety too. We are both vulnerable now.'

'Of course, I understand,' Melissa said, standing up. 'I'm scared shitless, Sister, if I'm honest. But I don't see how sending me home is going to make me any safer. If it's as dangerous around here as you say, and people have been watching our movements, then going home by myself makes me a sitting duck. I might as well write *Home alone, come and kill me* on my front door. If anyone wants to get me, I'll be playing right into their hands. And I've got nowhere else to go.' Fresh hot tears spilled from her eyes as she marched out of the room, shutting the door loudly behind her.

Immediately regretting how she'd handled the situation, Sister Veronica stared straight ahead, feeling the first real arrow of fear pierce through her habitually formidable reserve. This was a horrific state of affairs. There were no two ways about it, she and Melissa were now both in danger. With her heart racing faster by the second, she cursed the growing fear inside her, daring it to stop her from going forward, from continuing her investigation. But as she looked down and saw that her usually steady hands were shaking, a new wave of horror made her lean forwards, the understanding of the jeopardy she was now in causing nausea to rise.

8

———————

Feeling dispiritedly idle, Father Mathers poured himself another sweet sherry. That inconsequential little nun, Sister Veronica, was a pain in his side. It was her fault he'd started drinking before lunchtime again, and to think, he'd nearly managed to get out of that habit. She was like a terrier, always snapping at his heels, sniffing him out at the least convenient times. Why couldn't the woman learn her place? The sisters were volunteers, there to serve, and should only offer their opinion when called on. This was the natural order of things, it was divine law, it was what God had decreed when he made only men apostles. He was going to have to break the old dog's strong-mindedness somehow.

Honestly, the woman was odious, far too smart. Her opinions were coarse, her comments too direct. She had no understanding of social nuances, it was uncouth and embarrassing. And to think that he, Zachary Mathers, who had risen to the rank of diocesan priest exceptionally quickly and now considered Cardinal Moore – the prince of the Catholic Church in Britain – a personal friend, should have to put up with this kind of behaviour from a female. It was distasteful; it maligned his sense of worth.

He was sure she'd overheard him talking in the convent the other day. Nosy old crow. He hadn't been doing anything wrong, and his business was none of hers anyway. Then, of course, she was there to upset His Eminence when the wretched boy's body was discovered yesterday. It was a damn shame, of course, the whole affair. But His Grace was right, it had to be dealt with internally, there was no question of that. He completely understood why the Cardinal had bestowed on him the responsibility of making sure she kept that bleating mouth of hers firmly shut. What he needed to do was to give the woman a bloody good fright. Take her down a step or two. Didn't the Early Church Fathers identify women as the cause of evil entering the world? That race were lucky they'd been given a place in the Roman Catholic Church at all. As his wise old mother had always said, women should ultimately always defer to men. And she always knew best, God rest her soul.

He sipped his sherry and leaned back in his antique chair – being careful not to disturb his meticulously parted tresses – trying to shut irritating images of the old busybody out of his mind. His sleek black cat, Tertullian, eyed him lazily from the chaise longue on the other side of the room. After all, Father Mathers consoled himself, he'd already become accustomed to mixing within far higher circles. Soon, if all went to plan, he wouldn't have to see much of those tweed-skirted sisters down the street at all. Anxieties flooded his mind as he went through the logistics of what he needed to do. He, Father Zachary St John Mathers, a distinguished scholar and devout religious minister, deserved more in life and he was bloody well going to make sure he got it.

The telephone rang. Father Mathers rose gracefully from his chair.

'Hello, Father Mathers speaking.'

'I'm getting worried,' a familiar voice said. 'You're running out of time, and nothing's happening. I'm worried you're going to break the deal.'

'I'm not going back on the deal,' Father Mathers shouted. The fingers of his left hand went immediately to his temple. 'I've told you before, I just need more time.'

He slammed the phone down.

It rang again.

'Listen, will you just–'

'Ah, good afternoon, Bishop Hammett here.' Father Mathers' blood pressure decreased. Ah, the Cardinal's secretary. After all, they were all working together now, weren't they? 'His Eminence has requested your presence at the Archbishop's House soon as possible, and asks if you could be on your way this very minute, with haste?'

'Of course, please tell His Grace I'll leave now,' Father Mathers said.

'Excellent. God bless.'

'God bless you, Father.'

Father Mathers gave a small smile as he put the phone down and treated himself to one last glass of sherry. An idea had just occurred to him that – if put into play – would certainly hamper Sister Veronica's nose for interference. He had a feeling he might share it with Cardinal Moore that very afternoon. That other bastard could wait. With renewed vigour, he swallowed, placed the empty glass down and reached for his briefcase.

9

It was with relief that Sister Veronica sat down to lunch; leek and potato soup and a wholemeal roll, prepared today by Sister Maria. By godfathers, she needed some sustenance and a minute or two of inconsequential chit-chat with the other sisters. Emotionally battered and bruised, she now had a resolute purposefulness goading her to look deeper into Jamie's death, and hang the consequences. If she could do this one useful thing with her life, even if it got her into trouble, then so be it; her existence would mean something in the end. But this moment of reprieve was gratefully received, a fleeting experience of familiarity before she descended into the turmoil of murder again. Even Sister Irene's expounding of her delight at the Vatican's most recently made saint – anything Sister Irene said usually had the effect of a cheese-grater on her nerves – was strangely comforting.

Melissa was not at lunch, she noticed, but Sister Veronica had not expected her to be. She'd handled the situation badly, she knew that, she'd said the wrong thing to the girl, silly woman. She'd been too overbearing when what the girl needed was understanding and a patient ear. But how did one handle trauma in the right way? No excuses, Veronica. Eat your food, then go and see Melissa and apologise.

Sister Mary was nodding along to Sister Irene's words.

'Papal supremacy is at the heart of my life,' Sister Mary joined in, tearing her roll in half. 'The Pope has spoken and I will follow him.'

'God give us all the grace and humility to honour His Holiness.' Sister Irene put her spoon down and bowed her head. 'We are but sheep in his flock, and we must listen to our shepherd.'

Sister Catherine chuckled.

'He's a very wealthy shepherd,' she said. 'I caught a headline on my way back from the soup kitchen yesterday. It said "Vatican's Wealth Runs to Billions".'

'Catherine!' Sister Irene's head snapped up. 'As you well know, the Vatican's wealth is not disposable, these reports are mythical. Our dear church runs more hospitals and charity than any other religion in the world with its investments. I highly recommend you read the Catholic social doctrine before making light of His Holiness's resources.'

'All right, calm down, Sister, my vocation is to serve the Pope too.' Sister Catherine grinned. 'Doesn't mean I can't mention the odd headline, does it, Veronica?'

Sister Veronica grunted. She had no intention of being drawn into any lunchtime politics today.

'Where's Sister Anastasia?' Sister Maria's girlish voice spoke out. 'Is she still unwell?'

'Sister Anastasia was taken to hospital last night,' Sister Julia, the Mother Superior, dragged herself from her melancholic reverie to speak. 'As most of you are aware, she was taken ill in the garden on the day of the carbon monoxide leak. She's been unable to speak since then, and last night her condition deteriorated. We will devote our afternoon prayers to her, of course.' Her hands groped the rosary around her neck, fingering the beads feverishly.

Sister Veronica sat up, surprised. Why hadn't she noticed poor Sister Anastasia was sick? Well, so much had happened, but still. She couldn't let her ties to her community slip. She was fond of the elderly nun, who'd always brought a grounding archaic air to the convent. She smiled, remembering their frequent chats about cricket, Sister Anastasia's favourite sport. The old nun couldn't watch it now, of course – having succumbed to glaucoma years ago – but she listened avidly to radio reports whenever she could, then relished a dissection of the scores with anyone who was free to chat. And she never complained about her eyesight, just incorporated her blindness into life quietly and stoically, always politely thanking the sisters when they looked after her. Why does it often take an illness for you to realise how much you value someone? Sister Veronica wondered, quietly sending up a prayer for her friend's recovery.

The rest of the meal passed in a staid unobtrusiveness, Sister Irene limiting herself to only occasional disapproving glances at Sister Catherine, who returned beaming smiles to her.

Sister Agnes gave her the odd encouraging grin from the opposite side of the table, which she returned each time, grimacing as best she could.

Father Adams, lapdog to Father Mathers, was sitting at the table too, hardly able to eat anything, which Sister Veronica supposed was due to nerves as it was his first time leading prayers at the convent that afternoon. His golden hair glittered in the sun's rays that shot through the kitchen window. When he asked Sister Maria to please pass the butter, her cheeks flushed scarlet. Good Lord, Sister Veronica said to herself. The man's unstoppable.

Just as she was wiping her mouth and intending to stand up

to help the rest of the sisters clear the table, Sister Julia slapped her hand down on it hard.

'A storm is coming,' the Mother Superior announced prophetically. 'I can feel it.' She put her hands to the air in the manner of a shamanic weather god.

'Oh for heaven's sake,' Sister Veronica muttered to herself, piling her soup bowl on top of others. 'She's so dramatic. You only have to look out of the window to see the clouds accumulating. Really!'

As she trudged up the flight of stairs towards Melissa's room, a plan of action formed in her mind. Perhaps she would share it with the girl, she wondered to herself. See what she thought? Maybe it would bond them together. Saints preserve her, she needed all the honest allies she could get at the moment. Up until now, she'd been approaching the whole debacle from the wrong angle, she'd realised. But now she knew what to do.

Puffing, as she arrived outside Melissa's door, Sister Veronica knocked three times. No answer. She cleared her throat loudly.

'Hello?' she called. 'Melissa, can I come in? I'm awfully sorry about before.'

Still no answer.

A feeling of dread coursed through her. Suddenly expecting the worst, a flashback of Jamie's body in her mind, Sister Veronica threw the door open.

The room was empty, bare. The girl had gone. No personal possessions or the merest hint of Melissa left behind at all, other than the lingering scent of musky perfume.

Entering the room, Sister Veronica picked up the piece of paper on the bed.

'Dear Mother Superior,' she read. 'Thank you so much for letting me stay in your convent, I have hugely enjoyed my time here. Unfortunately, I had a bad asthma attack this morning, and my Ventolin is running low, so I need to go and get this sorted out. Apologies for my sudden departure, but I hope you understand. I've done enough research here for the article, which I promise will portray the sisters in a positive light. I've taken my phone from the desk drawer in the office – please don't be cross. Thanks again and warmest regards to you all, Melissa.'

Damn, dash and blast, and double drat.

10

Cardinal Moore rested both elbows on his desk and leaned forward. In front of him, sat two gentlemen, their countenances mild, both dressed conservatively. Sister Bernadette – reassigned from the Convent of the Christian Heart to the Archbishop's House six years ago due to her utterly discretionary nature – had just served them tea. Now they were alone, the door shut. An observer would have had no hint of any interrogatory undertones to the meeting, it was a civilised assembly between men of God.

'I wanted to take this opportunity to ask how the investigation is going?' Cardinal Moore said.

'Very well, Your Eminence,' one of the men replied. His suit was cut by the best tailor in Savile Row.

'Wonderful. May I conclude that no trace of evidence was left at the scene?' Cardinal Moore's calculating mind was exposed. He wanted to guard against any future unsavoury surprises.

'Nothing at all. We collected all the evidence, and have disposed of it in the usual way. The builders at the hostel have been reinstated, paid more for their quick return. They are pouring rubble into the back garden as we speak,' the other man replied, his tone flat and professional.

'Perfect.'

They all sipped their tea.

'The second stage of the plan begins immediately,' Cardinal Moore said. 'As before, there can be no mistakes.'

'There won't be.'

'Is the team assembled?'

'Of course, already in place, and under our surveillance.'

'Very good.' Cardinal Moore betrayed no hint of emotion. He rarely did. 'How did the family take it?'

'They complied.'

'Good. Remember, all humans have limitations. Make sure no one's emotional frailties hamper the operation at any stage.'

'Of course, Your Grace. We are efficient at what we do.'

'I know you are,' the Cardinal murmured. He had worked with these men before. But warnings never went amiss, even with consummate professionals. It kept them on their toes. So he continued: 'However – just to clarify – if events did go wrong, alternative, ah, interventions would be swiftly made.'

The men nodded. They knew what this meant.

The man on the left retrieved a plain folder from his briefcase, and slid it across the table.

'Your paperwork, Your Eminence.'

'Excellent.' The Cardinal smiled faintly, appearing far younger than his sixty-six years. He flicked open the folder's cardboard flap and saw a ticket for a return flight to Rome. He glanced at his watch. That man Mathers should be arriving any minute. He allowed his smile to stretch wider. Life was most definitely like a board game, he felt. Chess would be the closest analogy. And Mathers was a weak piece; a pawn. A useful one, but still a pawn. The Cardinal closed the meeting with swiftness and expertise.

11

Father Mathers looked around at the elegant space Sister Bernadette had ushered him into. So much thought had gone into this room. The furniture, the wallpaper, the lighting, it was all so magnificent, so tasteful; so understated yet opulent. He licked his lips. One day, perhaps he might– He chuckled. Don't get ahead of yourself, old boy. One step at a time.

He'd hugely enjoyed strutting into the Archbishop's House, past that downtrodden wretch, Sister Cecelia who was mopping the floor, past Fathers Adebayo and Wade who were sitting behind the reception desk, and past the Cardinal's most trusted friend and his chief of staff and strategy, Bishop Sabell, who'd stared at him in the most unfriendly way. He hadn't cared a jot about how anyone looked at him. He, Father Mathers, was on the way up and no mistake.

While he waited, he adopted different sitting positions on the sofa, wondering which made him appear the most authoritative yet at the same time humbly servile and ingratiating. He was just in the middle of a position change when the door opened.

'Ah, Father Mathers.' The Cardinal had put on his robes

especially. He understood Mathers' admiration of status and possessions perfectly. 'So good of you to come.'

'Of course, Your Grace. I would do anything for you.'

'That really is the most marvellous news.' Cardinal Moore smiled as he sat down. 'Stuffy weather today?'

'Yes, at least we've had no more rain. The forecast says thunderstorms later.'

'Oh dear, how trying,' the Cardinal said. 'Listen, Father. The private investigation into the poor boy's murder is going well. Of course, the welfare of the boy's family is at the forefront of everything; the parents have been informed, and reassured that justice will be served.'

Father Mathers nodded sagely.

'I've just been rather concerned,' Cardinal Moore went on, 'about the poor nun who found the boy's body. What was her name?'

'Sister Veronica, Your Eminence. I was actually going to speak to–'

'Ah, yes, Sister Veronica,' the Cardinal said. 'She was so distraught, was she not? So traumatised by her finding? And understandably so. She's a woman, a being with a sensitive soul.'

Father Mathers nodded slowly. As well as a stab of irritation at not being able to fully explain and take credit for his idea, he was beginning to think the Cardinal may have already thought along the same lines.

'Her near hysteria led me to believe, upon reflection, that in due course she may benefit from a rest somewhere,' the Cardinal went on, his brow creased with concern. 'I believe it is very relaxing in the north of England?'

Father Mathers nodded seriously.

'I had already thought,' he couldn't help saying, 'that the poor woman could also do with, er, unwinding somewhere very far from London.'

'Ah, you know what they say about great minds.' Cardinal Moore allowed his eyes to widen a fraction with conspiratorial suggestion. 'Father Mathers, I believe you, with your understanding of the situation, are the perfect person to engage Mother Superior at the convent in a dialogue about Sister Veronica's health, forthwith. Of course, Sister Julia does not know about the boy, only about your carbon monoxide story, and that's all she needs to know. Please let her know that I've spoken to a convent in Cumbria, and that they will have room for Sister Veronica to join them in a week. Of course, this is in the poor woman's interests; she's suffered a terrible shock and needs to recuperate.' He allowed himself a concerned frown. 'Do pass on how concerned I was about the state of the poor nun's health when we visited the hostel to discuss a possible media engagement the other day. Positive promotion of the church is no longer a suitable possibility, of course, under present circumstances.' The briefest glimmer of irritation flickered across his eyes. 'Sister Veronica would clearly benefit from a permanent change of scene. Do you see?'

'Of course, Your Grace. It is my pleasure to serve you in any way I can. I have been very worried about Sister Veronica's health myself, and I am so pleased you are doing what is best for her.'

'Excellent.' Cardinal Moore stood up. 'Your service has been noted and will be duly rewarded.'

A thrill of delight ran down Father Mather's spine.

12

That afternoon, at the same time as Father Mathers was hailing a taxi back to Soho – the Cardinal hadn't offered his private driver for the return journey – Sister Veronica rocked backwards and forwards as the underground train built up speed. Wedged into the narrow seat, unable to shift into a more comfortable position, she glared at the girl covered in tattoos opposite her. The girl shot her a kind smile before staring back at her phone. So she glowered instead at the adverts above the girl's head. From the corner of her eye she detected a couple in a passionate embrace, swaying to and fro with the motion of the train. She hadn't been on the Tube for a while, she'd forgotten about its all-pervading stink of grime. Dash it all, why was she feeling so hostile? So belligerent? She wasn't usually like this. The desperation she felt about Jamie must be fuelling an anger that was bubbling up inside her, she decided.

On her way into the Tube station she'd passed a rack of daily newspapers, and caught a small headline on the front of *The Telegraph*: 'Cardinal Moore Promises Clerical Celibacy Will Never End'. Why say such a thing? Why was the man so against change? She couldn't help feeling it was a message to Jamie's father and people like him. Or maybe to those in the church who wanted the archaic rules relaxed.

Finding Melissa's address had been easy. As afternoon prayers began, she'd been in the convent office, snooping through the drawers, finding the book containing visitors' contact details. Sister Irene's inevitable wrath at her lack of appearance in prayers, and Mother Superior's inevitable despondent disappointment in her when Sister Irene complained, were no longer future events she cared about.

She was used to travelling on the underground, of course, in fact she considered herself a dab hand at it and purposefully never looked at the Tube maps as she passed them, choosing to turn her head nonchalantly the other way. Only Sister Irene, and until she was taken ill, Sister Anastasia, were virtual prisoners inside the convent. Sister Irene out of choice, she devoted her free time to prayer – apparently – and Sister Anastasia because she was wheelchair-bound.

Patience and saints preserve her, the rattling on this Tube was enough to give anyone an aneurism. Why hadn't she had the intelligence to ask Melissa what she knew about Jamie's father when she'd had the chance?

'Excuse me.' A wrinkled hand was laid on her arm. Sister Veronica snapped round to stare at its owner, who turned out to be a very old man. More hair escaped from her already wispy bun. She hadn't worn a habit for years and didn't intend to start up again now, but one thing they were good for, in her opinion, was for keeping hairstyles in place. Oh well. She'd just have to invest in some new clips and pins. 'I hope you don't mind me asking this,' he went on, 'but are you a nun?'

'Yes I am, as a matter of fact.'

'I knew it! It was your cross and your sandals that gave you away. I'm a Catholic too, Sister.'

Sister Veronica stared down at her plain brown sandals. She'd never considered them to be particularly 'nunnish'.

'I saw His Holy Father in Rome last year,' the old man said with a nostalgic smile. 'Best moment of my life.'

Sister Veronica stared at him.

'The Pope truly is a gift from our heavenly father, isn't he?' the man went on. 'All priests are really. I go and confess my sins every week, and I love absolution, when Father speaks for God, and tells me that God has forgiven me.'

Is that really all it takes? Sister Veronica wondered, as the train wobbled round a sharp bend. Can someone just confess murder to God, and God forgives him? I fear we've stopped using our brains in this world.

Twenty minutes later she stood, wheezing heavily, outside a baby-blue front door – 2B, Briar Mews – in Putney. Would the girl even open the door to her? There was only one way to find out. She rapped loudly, trying to shake off the unsettling feeling that she'd been followed since leaving the underground station.

13

Melissa stretched a long soapy leg upwards. Although she'd been kicking herself for flouncing out of the convent, soaking in this hot bath covered in Laura Mercier honeyed bath foam felt bloody good. Some of the traumatic burden she'd carried since this morning was easing; not leaving as such, just settling into something more manageable.

Well, she thought, your resolve didn't last long, did it, Melissa? One minute you were in it for the long haul, the next you storm out as soon as a nun says something you don't like. Grow up, girl, it's about time. Knee-jerk reactions had always been one of her weaknesses.

After a few more minutes, she rinsed her hair, then stepped out of the bath, wrapping herself up in a freshly-washed deep-pile towel. The smaller towel was wound round her head, turban-style.

She stared at herself in the mirror. Her spray tan was fading, and a new wrinkle had appeared. Other than that, things could be worse. She put her nose and eyebrow studs back in; banished during her time in the convent. Weird how it felt like a part of her was missing without them these days.

Going into her bedroom, she grabbed her phone and thumbed through her playlist. What she needed was some loud indie funk. My Baby's 'In the Club' soon swung through the room. As she pulled on her skinny jeans and white shirt, and thrust her feet into her pale-blue sliders, she tilted her head. Was that someone knocking at her door? Bloody hell, whoever it was was giving her door knocker a run for its money.

She took a quick peek through the eyehole, then opened the door.

'Sister Veronica!'

'I was beginning to worry you weren't in,' the old nun said, looking over her shoulder quickly.

'I'm so sorry–' Melissa started at the same time as Sister Veronica said,

'About this morning, I need to apologise.'

They stared at each other and grinned, the air between them now peaceful. It felt good to be smiling about something for a moment.

'Come in, Sister, come and have a cup of tea.' Melissa held the door wide open. 'I can't believe you travelled all the way out here to find me.'

'Well...' Sister Veronica tried to drag her gaze away from the newly arrived metalwork on Melissa's face. 'There are lots of questions I need to ask you, my dear. I would love a cup of tea – three sugars – if you don't mind.'

Melissa's ground-floor apartment was small but stylish, Sister Veronica thought as she heard the girl flip the kettle on in the kitchen. She had a good look round at the pots of ferns, the large Lichtenstein pop art print on the wall, the two laptops – why did the girl need two? – both in baby pink, and the smart corner-sofa suite. A large ashtray – empty – on a side table, with a box of nicotine patches next to it. The walls, painted a pale-teal colour, made the room soothing to be in. She was glad to see a well-stocked bookshelf. Excellent. The girl was a reader. She'd been right to trust her.

Melissa smiled as she came back carrying two steaming mugs.

'Here you go.' She placed one on the rosewood coffee table in front of the nun, before settling back into the armchair.

'Marvellous, thank you.' Sister Veronica took a noisy sip. 'Now, what I should have asked you earlier, but didn't, was what you know about the identity of Jamie's father?'

'Nothing, I'm afraid.' Melissa's face creased with the effort of trying to recall any helpful information. 'I literally just got a message from Children of the Blessed, that's the French support group, saying that Jamie Markham was the child of a priest and was in Westminster. The group might know more though. Look, I'll show you their internet site.'

She grabbed one of the pink laptops and pulled up a webpage.

'Look, Sister.'

The old nun leaned forward and took the laptop.

'And you're in touch with this group?'

'Yes, I speak to the founder a few times a week. He's been great actually.'

'Do you think you could introduce me to them? We need to find out as much as we can about Jamie, and the most key information is about his father. I can go and talk to his mother, of course, but I have a feeling the Cardinal will have silenced the woman somehow.'

'Sister,' Melissa said. 'It's an utterly horrific possibility that

Jamie might have been murdered by someone inside the church, and I think that idea has come to both of our minds many times. But have you considered that maybe Jamie was killed by someone unconnected to the church?'

'Yes, yes I have, that definitely needs to be considered.' Sister Veronica shook her head then frowned. 'But I just can't fully accept it as a probability. It seems too much of a coincidence that he'd come to find his father here, that it was a secret he was planning to share.'

A thought occurred to Melissa, and she mulled it over for a second or two. Would it work or was she being overly spontaneous? While in private she took ages to trust people, in her professional life her spontaneity was legendary, and she was itching to get out of London...

'Er, Sister Veronica,' she said. 'This might sound a bit much, but my brother – also adopted – lives in Paris. He's an artist in residence at a gallery there.'

'The Louvre?' Sister Veronica's eyes widened. She recalled a much enjoyed break in Paris with Sister Agnes, and how they'd marvelled at the paintings by the old masters for hours in the Louvre. Even then they hadn't seen all there was, the building was enormous. In the end Sister Agnes' legs had ached so much so they'd found a café for respite, but oh how she would love to return one day and finish her tour.

'No, he's good but he's not that good.' Melissa smiled. 'He works in a smaller gallery in Montmartre. Now, I haven't told my editor that I've left the convent yet, so I'm basically a free woman for the next four days, until Monday. I know it's probably a crazy idea, but we could get a Eurostar over to Paris and I could introduce you to the group. I've always wanted to meet them in person.' And I could do with getting away for a day or two, she added privately. I need to get some perspective on all this craziness. 'If they have any documents about him, like copies of birth certificates, photos, or anything, then they will be able to show you in person. They always ask each priest or nun's child for as much information as possible.'

Sister Veronica frowned.

'Just go to Paris?' She was trying to work out the logistics. Easter week was out of the way – it had come early this year – so she had no pressing responsibilities other than her normal chores. And now that the students in the Catholic hostel had been rehoused...

'It would be helpful, vital in fact, to see any documents that connect Jamie with his father,' she said. 'But I don't know if Mother Superior would grant me permission, after all, she doesn't know that Jamie is dead and on no account can I tell her. And I'm not exactly her favourite person, Sister Irene makes sure of that.'

'Oh Sister Irene, she's hard work, isn't she?' Melissa rolled her eyes. 'She kept telling me that a woman's place is in the home, not out at work. I don't think she approves of me at all.'

Sister Veronica grimaced.

'I tell you what,' she said. 'Can you let me mull the Paris idea over for a day or two? Are you sure your brother won't mind? If you give me your number, I'll see what I can do about getting permission to leave for a couple of days, but I have a feeling it won't come to pass. No one in my convent likes change, and as such, travelling usually takes an age to organise.'

Melissa took her notebook out of her handbag, wrote her number down, trying to ignore the slight pang of disappointment she felt. For a moment, she'd been visualising herself and Sister Veronica zooming over to Paris – travelling first class, of course – finding time to visit several cafés en route to speak with Children of the Blessed. But, of course, in reality, Sister Veronica couldn't just up and leave on a whim. After all, she – Melissa – might be able to extract any information that they needed from the support group's founder over the phone. Perhaps that's what her new friend was hoping for but was too polite to ask. She ripped out the page from her notebook, and Sister Veronica folded it and put it in the depths of her carrier bag.

'No, Sean won't mind, he's always trying to get me to go and visit, but I keep saying I'm too busy,' she said with a smile.

She watched Sister Veronica thumb through the pages of the black diary she'd retrieved from her bag.

'Melissa, this is Jamie's diary,' Sister Veronica said. 'I took it out of his room after I knew the Cardinal was going to try and cover up his murder. On the day he was killed, Jamie was expecting me to come over and bake my usual cake. All it says on that day, is *Today's the day: Tell Sister Veronica*. What do you think he meant by that?'

'I reckon he was planning to tell you about his father,' Melissa said. 'It's a big deal being the child of a priest or a nun, it's like you have to come out about it to your friends and family who don't know. My friend Andre from the group, is also the child of a priest, and he said it was easier to come out as gay to his friends than it was to tell them about his dad.'

Sister Veronica nodded, her jowly cheeks wobbling.

'Yes, I felt he was going to disclose information about his father to me too,' she said. 'In his room he had so many packets of pills. Do you know what Sertraline is? Or what Lithium is used for?'

'Sertraline is an antidepressant,' Melissa said. 'The doctor put me on it once a few years ago when the relationship with my adoptive mum started going bad. I just felt so low at the time.'

'Oh dear, that sounds most wearisome.' Sister Veronica took a swig of her tea. 'Are things better now?'

'I'm not depressed anymore, Sister, if that's what you mean. But no, my mother and I don't talk. She knows who my birth mother is, but she's refusing to tell me because she doesn't want me to make trouble for the church. She'll protect them at all costs.' Melissa looked down. 'That's one of the reasons Sean went to France, he can't handle her either. She's so miserable about everything all the time.'

'Well, she's lucky to have a daughter like you,' Sister Veronica said stoutly.

Melissa smiled.

'I've never taken Lithium, but I think it's used to help people with bipolar disorder,' she said. The nun looked blank. 'Manic depression,' Melissa added. There was no way she was going to tell the old girl about all the less legal chemicals she'd experimented with at uni.

'Oh poor boy, he was in a bad way.' Sister Veronica shook her head sorrowfully. 'Is there anything else, anything at all that you can think of that might help Jamie?'

'Only putting you in touch with the support group,' Melissa said. 'Sorry, Sister, I keep kicking myself for not going to see him earlier. But if anyone knows anything about him, it will be Children of the Blessed. I'll phone them and see if they'll talk to you.'

She reached for her mobile and found the number. It rang and rang.

'There's often no answer during the day,' she said. 'All the people who work at the group hold down jobs and run the group in the evenings. I'll keep trying.'

She saw the old nun glance at her digital wall clock.

'I must be going,' Sister Veronica said. 'I want to pop in at the hospital on the way back and see Sister Anastasia. The poor thing collapsed the other day, it must be the heat. And I need to get back before dinner, Sister Irene is going to make such a fuss as it is.' She heaved herself up.

'You've got my number.' Melissa didn't want the nun to go,

she realised. It felt safer with her there. 'Call me if I can help at all, okay?'

'Thank you, you've been so helpful already, my dear. If your support group will talk to me, please call the convent office and leave a message for me to phone you back. Walls have ears in that place, one can never be too careful. If the group have any information about Jamie at all, it would be marvellous.' Sister Veronica turned and waved. 'Look after yourself, and put that chain on your door at night.'

14

The interior of Westminster's Holy Cross Chapel was cool and dark. Bishop Hammett walked down the aisle and round the apse, not giving one glance to the glazed depictions of saints in the stained-glass windows. He'd studied them hundreds of times before. Today, his destination was the intricately-carved confessional near the crypt.

He entered the small dark space, knelt, and made the sign of the cross, feeling tears already wetting his eyes.

'Bless me, Father, for I have sinned,' he said to the obscured latticed window. Only a silhouette and a grunt confirmed the presence of the other. 'It has been three days since my last confession, and again, I want to declare my weakness, for it is a weakness, for the flesh of another.'

Another grunt.

'I confess that I have had impure thoughts about this person, and some acts of togetherness with them.'

A moment of silence from the other side. Then a man's voice spoke:

'The flesh is weak, Father. You must pray to the God

Almighty for guidance and strength, it is the devil throwing temptation in your path.'

'I will.' Bishop Hammett was sobbing now. 'I will continue to pray. But, Father, I don't have the strength to resist. My God, I am sorry for my sins with all my heart. In choosing to do wrong and failing to do good, I have sinned against you who I should love above all things. I firmly intend, with your help, of course, to do penance, to not sin anymore, and to avoid whatever leads me to sin. Our Saviour Jesus Christ suffered and died for us. In his name, my God, have mercy.'

He heard a sigh. Then the unseen man spoke again:

'I see. God, the Father of mercies, through the death and resurrection of his Son has reconciled the world to himself and sent the Holy Spirit among us for the forgiveness of sins, through the ministry of the church may God give you pardon and peace, and I absolve you from your sins in the name of the Father, and of the Son, and of the Holy Spirit. Go in peace.'

'Thank you, Father. Thanks be to God.' Bishop Hammett crossed himself and stood up.

Calmer now, forgiven, he walked back up the same aisle, his head bowed. He crossed himself again before leaving the chapel.

Blinking, as the bright sun hit him, his thoughts turned to Father Mathers. He'd been concealed in a side room when the man had arrived at the Archbishop's House yesterday. He'd seen him, of course, through the crack in the door. He'd almost been able to smell the odour of pompousness that the man carried around with him like a bad aftershave. Although he didn't like the ferrety-faced priest, he felt he should be almost grateful to him. After all, he'd been an unexpected decoy, allowing Bishop Hammett to gain access to strictly confidential information.

It had been unusual for His Eminence to leave such a private folder on his desk, usually everything of significance was locked in his impenetrable filing cabinet. Bishop Hammett supposed it was the early arrival of Father Mathers that had thrown His Grace somewhat, making him exit his office with haste. Of course he – Bishop Hammett – had looked through the file, making sure the door was firmly shut first. Sister Bernadette was the Cardinal's personal sniffer dog. The contents had not surprised him; after all, he was a priest with as much complex knowledge of the secret Catholic underworld as most who'd risen to his station. The information had been helpful though. He now knew what he needed to do next.

15

Shifting her carrier bag to the other hand, Sister Veronica entered South Kensington's hospital, St George's, the smooth sliding doors closing neatly behind her. Sweating profusely, she thanked God for the chilled air that immediately surrounded and cooled her. She looked up as thunder cracked overhead; she'd made it just in time to miss the rain.

The astonishingly young receptionist – she didn't look a day over sixteen – sent her off towards Sister Anastasia's ward with a small smile and tired eyes. Approaching the old nun's bed, she saw a most welcome figure already there, head bowed in prayer.

'Father John!'

'Sister, at last! I was hoping to see you.' His kind eyes wrinkled as he looked up. 'How on earth are you after the whole carbon monoxide affair? Please, have this seat.'

After Sister Veronica had sat down and they'd exchanged pleasantries, and Father John had gone off in search of a second uncomfortable chair, Sister Veronica bent over Sister Anastasia. She was shocked at what she saw. The old nun was asleep, God bless her, her pallid face sunken unusually at one side. Someone had taken her habit off, and her sparse white hair stuck up in tufts all over her head.

'The doctor said she's suffered a stroke,' Father John said as he returned, placing a chair down. 'He said this often happens to very old people in strong heat. She's been asleep for most of the time I've been here, poor old Anastasia.'

They bowed their heads, Sister Veronica praying fervently that her Sister felt no pain.

'Father Mathers was in full micro-managing mode the other day.' Father John smiled after a few moments. 'He sent me away like a naughty schoolboy, told me not to ask any questions.'

Sister Veronica couldn't help smiling.

'I can quite imagine him doing that. That man's a menace.' Then she looked away, wishing she could tell her friend more. She was glad to see him, but at the same time it made her feel lonely, reinforcing the fact that she had to carry the burden of Jamie's murder silently.

'Are you all right, Veronica? You look sad.' Father John leaned forward, concerned. 'I know you well enough to know when something's up. Sister Irene's not being difficult again is she?'

'Oh it's just–' Sister Veronica began, then stopped. 'I just feel let down by something, John. And I've had a busy day in this sweltering heat. It all gets a bit much for an old goose like me.'

'Let me find you some water.' Father John stood up and went off on his mission, she heard him asking one of the nurses if there was a water cooler about.

Sister Anastasia made a gurgling noise, bringing Sister Veronica to her feet at once.

'Hello, my dear. It's me, Veronica. How are you today?' She stroked a tuft of the old nun's hair. Sister Anastasia's blind eyes opened.

'I know,' the nun whispered. At least that's what it sounded like, her speech was so slurred.

'What do you know?' Sister Veronica asked, bending down.

The old nun's mouth moved in a variety of directions as she tried to form words.

'I know,' she repeated at last. 'Wha happened tha day.'

Sister Veronica's heart lurched. She immediately thought of Jamie, then berated herself for linking everything with him. The old nun was probably just confused. But what if she was trying to tell her something significant? This would be her only chance to find out. Her brain raced; where had Sister Anastasia been at the time of his murder? She didn't know the precise time the boy had been killed, but he'd been alive that morning – the other hostel students had told Melissa they remembered seeing him. And she'd found him dead at half past three. She remembered hearing voices in the convent garden as she got the cake ingredients together in the kitchen, and she recalled thinking that one or other of the sisters usually wheeled Anastasia into the garden to sleep in the sun.

'What happened with what?' Sister Veronica asked, looking around, hoping the old nun would speak again before Father John got back.

Again, her mouth made shapes, her lips pressed together. She was desperately trying to say something. Sister Veronica leaned forward even further.

'M-m-m-m-murder,' Sister Anastasia said slowly. Then her eyes closed.

'Here we are,' Father John said cheerfully, as he victoriously carried in two plastic cups of water.

'Thank you, John,' Sister Veronica said distractedly, her mind working overtime.

'Did she say anything while I was gone?'

'What? Oh, no, no, just some gurgling noises,' Sister

Veronica said, taking a quick sip of water. 'I think she's gone back to sleep. I must go now, John, or Sister Irene will have me hauled up in front of the Cardinal for negligence of my vows.'

Father John smiled.

'It's been good to see you, Veronica,' he said. 'Take care of yourself, you look tired.'

Fifty minutes later, Sister Veronica trudged heavily down Soho Street towards Soho Square Gardens. The storm had passed, leaving a pale dusky sky and glistening pools of water on the pavements in its wake. All she could do, she considered, glancing at a wispy white cloud, was to carry on, do her best for Jamie, and hope and pray that things got easier from here. It would be some consolation to help bring justice for Jamie, if indeed she could.

As she neared the intersection, a woman came towards her.

'Sister Cecelia?' Sister Veronica was surprised, but she was so tired she could hardly get the words out. 'What are you doing here?' Sister Cecelia worked for the Cardinal in the Archbishop's House. She'd always seemed like a downtrodden doormat, unlike that Sister Bernadette.

'I've been asked to deliver this to you.' The nun thrust forward a white envelope.

Sister Veronica looked at the writing on the front. It was written in capitals, but the handwriting still looked vaguely familiar. She ripped it open, pulled out the folded white sheet, and read: 'Sister Veronica, I write to you as a friend. Information has come to me that Cardinal Moore is planning to have you moved to a closed convent in the north. He is worried you might talk about the affair with Jamie Markham. Father Mathers has been speaking to Sister Julia about it this afternoon. I urge you to hastily rehouse yourself before this happens. Justice needs to be served. From a concerned sympathiser.'

'Who gave you this?' Sister Veronica demanded sharply. But

Sister Cecelia shook her head as she scurried away. She stared back at the note. Dash it all, where did she recognise that writing from? Someone with inside knowledge wrote this, but it wasn't the Cardinal or Father Mathers, that was for sure, and apart from Melissa, Sister Anastasia and herself she hadn't thought anyone else knew about Jamie. But the tangled secret web of the church's underbelly was obviously more complex than she knew. So many secrets and so many lies, it was disturbing. Whoever it was seemed to want to help her, and they had given her an idea.

As she entered the convent the first thing she saw was Sister Irene's intensely smug face. How long had the old goat been standing there?

'Mother Superior would like to see you in her office, Sister. Now.'

Sister Veronica entered the office and sat down in the worn-looking swivel chair opposite Sister Julia.

'Sister Veronica.' Sister Julia's serious face studied her own. 'Today has been full of people giving me reports about you. First, Father Mathers tells me that both himself and His Eminence are concerned that you are under undue mental stress, following your recent meeting with them. Apparently, you exhibited near hysterical behaviour, although I find this hard to imagine. Then Sister Irene tells me that not only have you missed yet another prayer meeting, but that you left the convent today without asking permission, and were gone for hours.' She stopped, considering the hot-looking, dishevelled nun before her for a moment. 'Well?' she said. 'What have you got to say by way of explanation for all this?'

'I went to see Sister Anastasia in hospital this afternoon,' Sister Veronica said, quite truthfully, trying not to focus on the implications behind the words the old nun had uttered to her until she'd left the meeting. 'Father John was there. I'm sorry I didn't ask your permission, Sister, but the urge to visit Anastasia overtook me just as afternoon prayers were beginning, and I decided to follow my instincts and go. I was very anxious to see her soon, just in case her condition worsened and I didn't get another chance.'

'I see.' Sister Julia's shoulders stayed tense. 'And this nonsense about you being hysterical?'

'I honestly don't know what they mean by that,' Sister Veronica said. 'All I did that day was help Father Mathers pack up the students' belongings, and I did that very calmly, in my opinion.' She smiled.

Sister Julia sighed. Sister Veronica had never seen her look so concerned. Mother Superior's dramatic histrionics were far more preferable to the look of steady apprehension she was currently shooting in her direction. It was as though the woman could swing between acute academic soberness and flailing fervent drama at will, which was a most disquieting talent to inflict on those around as one never knew what to expect next.

'Veronica, this isn't the first time we've had a chat like this, is it?' A deep exhalation of breath.

'No, Sister.'

'I don't know what you've done to get on His Grace's radar, but whatever it is, I would suggest you stop it at once. Father Mathers – quite enthusiastically in my opinion – said that His Grace thinks it would be better to move you out of London, perhaps to a calmer setting in the north of England. It would be better for your nerves, apparently. You need to understand that as His Grace has decided this, it's out of my hands completely. You have to go, do you understand? I'm sorry, Veronica. Please behave with obedience from now on.'

'Yes, Mother Superior,' Sister Veronica said, standing up and smoothing down her skirt. 'Thank you, I understand.'

Up in her room, Sister Veronica rooted through the mess at

the bottom of her cupboard, digging downwards like an angry mole, sending possessions and knick-knacks flying.

A week? The Cardinal was moving her to an obscure convent in a week? Oh no, absolutely not. He wasn't getting rid of her that easily, thank you very much. She finally located her old satchel under a pile of winter clothes. Into it, went Jamie's diary, the stash of money she'd secretly been hoarding to buy books with, her passport – applied for three years ago when she'd gone to spend six weeks in a convent in Nairobi – two full packets of custard creams, a pen, clothing and the piece of paper with Melissa's number on it.

She made a great show of being at dinner that evening, chatting to Sister Mary about Nigeria, smiling at Agnes, ignoring Sister Irene, filling everyone in on the fact that poor Sister Anastasia had suffered a stroke and that when she'd left, Father John had been there, watching over her and praying.

The nuns generally went to bed early; they were all required to rise at dawn for morning prayers. By half past nine, everything was quiet. If the nuns weren't asleep, they were resting in their rooms. Sister Veronica picked up her satchel and her coat, and descended the stairs with what she hoped was stealth. Most of the lights in the halls were out, just the stairwell strip lighting cast dim hospital-like illumination down the corridors. Gentle snoring came from one of the rooms.

Achieving the ground floor without hearing anyone stir, Sister Veronica tiptoed into the office and placed a note on Mother Superior's desk. Then she unbolted the front door as quietly as she could, knowing the Chubb lock would automatically click and keep the sisters safe when she shut it again.

Setting off at an unusually smart pace, Sister Veronica headed up Soho Street towards London's busy Oxford Street.

She veered off into a busy café, and swung her crucifix out of her shirt so it was noticeable.

'Excuse me,' she shouted to the Polish waitress, desperate to be heard above the pounding music and rowdy customers. 'I'm from the convent in Soho Square Gardens. Our phone is broken, and one of the sisters has been taken ill. Could I possibly use your phone for a moment?' Honestly, Veronica, she warned herself, as she watched the waitress grab a phone. You'll be as bad as Father Mathers if you become any more proficient at lying. She had Melissa's number ready in her hand. Taking the phone into a corner of the café, she tapped the numbers in.

'Hello, Melissa? It's Sister Veronica. Something's happened. Yes, I'm fine. I can't explain at the moment but I would now most definitely like to take you up on your idea of going to Paris.'

16

Father Mathers' fingers drummed out an agitated beat on the back of the chair. He watched a series of muscles twitch down both sides of the Cardinal's face.

'Missing?' Cardinal Moore hissed. 'What do you mean, Sister Veronica is missing? How can a nun go missing?'

'I don't know, Your Grace. Like I said, Sister Julia telephoned me this morning in a panic. They've looked in Sister Veronica's room, and some of her belongings have gone too.' He tried to slow his breaths.

'Well where is she?'

'I-I-I don't know, Your Eminence.'

Father Mathers had to endure the sight of Cardinal Moore's lip curling contemptuously.

'This is your responsibility, Father.' Cardinal Moore's dark eyes lasered into his. 'All I asked you to do was to watch the nun and make sure she behaved. And now you tell me she's gone missing? This is not good enough. Find the woman. And bring her to me with the utmost urgency. Today. I have a pressing engagement in Rome that I cannot miss, and my flight leaves this evening. I want this disastrous matter cleared up well before that. Things will turn most unfortunate for you if you fall short this time. Do you understand?'

'Of course, Your Grace. I'm so sorry.'

'Then why are you still standing here?' The Cardinal's face twisted and he banged his fist on the desk. The controlled, sophisticated man had morphed into a tower of aggression, spittle wet his lips and his eyes blazed with fury.

'Go!' Cardinal Moore snarled. 'What the hell are you waiting for, man?'

Father Mathers ran his tongue round his dry mouth as he hurried out. It wasn't just Cardinal Moore that terrified him, it was also the much unwanted information Bishop Hammett had hissed into his ear on the way up. The bishop's instructions had been unthinkable, but what else was he supposed to do?

17

Melissa's feet tapped on the floor of the train, urging it to go faster. She stared through the window at the Paris suburbs, which were a more comforting sight than Sister Veronica's depressed face opposite her.

She couldn't deny that she'd felt a thrill of excitement when Sister Veronica had phoned last night, she'd felt like she was in an action-adventure film. Let's jump on a train to Paris? Sure, she could make that happen. She'd always been good at flying by the seat of her pants, that was one of the things that made her such an agile journalist; she'd throw herself into anything. A few phone calls later, she'd met Sister Veronica by the clock tower at King's Cross, they'd spent the night in a twin room in the Travelodge, discussing Sister Anastasia's revelations into the early hours, then had made it onto the Eurostar from St Pancras by half past seven that morning.

She sighed, tucking some strands of hair behind her ears. This would almost be fun if the purpose of their mission wasn't so awful, and if Sister Veronica wasn't so moody.

'A week, Melissa,' Sister Veronica said, yet again. Her eyebrows were so low they'd almost eclipsed her eyes. 'The man was going to transfer me in a week. Without consulting me, taking me away from everything and everyone I know. And him, a man of God!'

'It's just not fair, Sister,' Melissa soothed, adjusting her sleeve to hide her nicotine patch. 'But he won't get the chance now, you're with me now, and we are doing this for Jamie, aren't we? My brother said he's looking forward to meeting you. Children of the Blessed are based fairly close to where he lives, just a couple of stops away on the Metro. They said they will be happy to talk to you, they were horrified to hear what's happened to Jamie.'

Sister Veronica's eyes darted to and fro as the train zoomed on.

'This church has evil at its core, Melissa.'

'Yep,' Melissa agreed. 'I think lots of people see that, Sister. The way it tried to cover up the clerical sexual abuse crisis was terrible; I wrote an article about it. Lots of bishops and cardinals knew these children were being hurt but they did nothing to help them.'

'I thought the men who committed those crimes were bad apples,' Sister Veronica said. 'I knew there was corruption, but I thought it was contained, and getting better now that it was so public. But now I'm beginning to wonder whether that was just the tip of the iceberg. All these underhand dirty dealings, it's like the Mafia.'

'Apparently, the Vatican Bank does have links with the Mafia, I read that when I was writing the article,' Melissa said. 'But there are hundreds of good people like you in the church too, Sister. Don't forget that.'

'Yes, most of the people I know in the church are good people,' Sister Veronica said. 'But they are not the ones who hold the power, they are just following their vocations, trying to do their best, believing the drivel that those in power put out –

poor beggars – when in actual fact what seems to be happening is the cover-ups of crimes. And they are crimes,' she added vehemently. 'I don't care what the Cardinal says about sin; abuse and murder are crimes and it's not right to keep them secret just to save the face of an institution that clearly has corruption at its core. I'm no longer working for the Catholic Church, I'm working for God. And they are two very different things.'

Melissa nodded. She had grown very fond of this old lady over the last twenty-four hours. There was something very refreshing about Sister Veronica's ability to stare a problem in the face and honestly address it even when her view contrasted with her institution's.

'No one's pulled the wool over your eyes yet, though, have they, Sister?' She glanced out of the window. 'Ooh look, we're coming into Paris. Won't be long now.'

18

The chairman of Soho's St Joseph's parish church council, Martin O'Hara, paced the room. Why the fuck wasn't that priest, Mathers, answering his phone? He was late to their meeting, again. Would he fail to turn up, like last time? Mathers' recent behaviour was of grave concern to Martin. They'd done a deal, all in good faith, a little transfer of funds that benefited both of them and hurt no one. Martin had come good on his half, and Mathers had reaped the rewards, lots of them. But why wasn't he fulfilling what he'd promised? He'd left Martin in the shit and now pressure was mounting, the bursar had mentioned that there was a problem with the books, that the funds no longer added up. If there was an investigation there was no way he was going to take the rap for the priest, no way.

It was only half past ten, but Martin took his flask out of his bag and took a deep draught of scotch. He badly needed something to take the edge off, to calm his nerves. If he went down, the priest was sure as hell coming with him.

He reached for his phone, Mathers' number was at the top, of course. He tapped the button, listened, but the phone just rang and rang. He gulped more of his drink. He'd been waiting for Mathers for forty-five minutes. The priest wasn't coming, he could feel it in his bones.

Right. He'd had enough of the lying bastard. Time to take matters into his own hands.

19

'Can we call in on Sean before we go to the offices?' Melissa asked as they exited the Gare du Nord, breathing in the hustle and bustle of Paris life.

'Of course, let us go right away, does your brother know the time of our arrival?'

'I phoned and left a message.' Melissa smiled.

The taxi bombed through the crowded streets and Sister Veronica's breathing slowed as the distraction of Paris temporarily overtook her frazzled mind. As they alighted onto a cobbled street, she looked up at the beautiful terraced houses towering over the boulevard. Lines of washing fluttered over their heads and music and raised voices floated above the beeps from the now gridlocked traffic around them.

'He is on the third floor of this one.' Melissa pointed to an old wooden double door, with a line of bell pushes beside it.

She rang one and they heard a distant jangle.

'Oui?' a voice from above them called down.

'Sean, it's me!' Melissa stepped back into the street.

'Sis! Come on up, the door is open.'

The next half an hour became a blur of steep steps, joyful

introductions, hastily assembled refreshments, admiration of abstract paint-splattered depictions of the River Seine, and the alarming realisation that they were very soon due in nearby Notre Dame de Lorette. Ten minutes later, after a crowded Metro ride, Sister Veronica found herself seated in the shabby office rented by Children of the Blessed, quickly orientating herself.

She put down the fresh mug of coffee Melissa pushed into her hands and stared into Dominique Caron's beautiful, serious face.

'Thousands of priests' and nuns' children?' she repeated. 'All over the world? Are you sure?'

'Very sure, Sister,' Dominique said in her lilting English accent. 'We have been running this group for three years now, and we have evidence to show this. Thousands is a conservative estimate. In many countries like Nigeria and the Philippines, the priests have more than one child and live quite openly with them. The real number is probably nearer tens of thousands.'

'But why doesn't the world know about this?' Sister Veronica's brow furrowed.

'Because the church and their mothers and fathers, and also communities, silence them. They usually believe they are doing the best for the child.'

Sister Veronica nodded. She was thinking back to her own mother's words, 'We must protect the church's good name, Veronica... Just forget you ever found out, put it out of your mind, do you hear? I never want to hear another word about this.'

'Yes.' She nodded slowly. 'Yes, I see.'

'Jamie's case was textbook.' Dominique shook her head. 'He found out he'd been lied to all his life, that his real father was a priest, that he'd been fed made-up stories about his heritage just so his father could continue to be seen to be celibate.

Unfortunately, his mental health was very fragile. It all got too much for him and he tried to commit suicide. Unfortunately, this is normal for priests' children. The data we have, and the data we've been given from other countries, suggests that over fifty-five per cent of priests' and nuns' children will attempt suicide during their lives.'

Sister Veronica let the shock pass through her body.

'But why?' she asked. 'That number is staggeringly high.'

'Yes, it is,' Dominique agreed. 'There are a number of risk factors for priests' and nuns' children that contribute towards this. If someone has too many of these factors they are statistically more likely to attempt suicide or have suicide ideation. Poor Jamie had lots of these. He was once very devoutly Catholic, you know, so when he found out he felt the attached shame and stigma very strongly, he internalised it. He was lied to, his father rejected him. The church closed doors in his face when he went to them for help.'

Sister Veronica shook her head.

'This is inexcusable,' she said. 'Children should not be born into this.'

'I absolutely agree with you, Sister Veronica,' Dominique said. 'The church is known to have gone to extreme lengths to stop priests' and nuns' children from finding out about their parentage. We've been shown evidence of court cases, confidentiality agreements, destroyed birth certificates, lie upon lie upon lie. All to make priests and nuns appear celibate when they are not, and this is all to protect the good name of the church. Celibacy is one of the tenets that the church rotates around. If they are seen to be failing at this, the whole structure of it falls down. They are prepared to keep the image of priests and nuns being collectively celibate at all costs.'

Sister Veronica snorted.

'But murder?' she said. 'Have you seen that before?'

'I've heard of cases,' Dominique said darkly. 'Have you seen the documentary series called *The Keepers*? It's on Netflix.'

'What is Netflix?' Sister Veronica said. 'I've heard of it but I've no idea what it is.'

'Ah, your mind is purer than mine, Sister,' Dominique said. 'Netflix is a streaming service for televisions and other digital devices like laptops. You can watch films and documentaries on it. I have to admit, I watch it quite often in the evenings.'

'Me too,' Melissa said. 'I'm addicted.' Dominique smiled at her.

'*The Keepers* is a documentary series about the unsolved murder of Sister Cathy Cesnik, who strongly believed a priest at the school she taught in had committed awful sexual abuse crimes. Many people believe that Sister Cathy was murdered to silence her, to stop her talking about what the priest had done, and that the church covered this up. So you see, there are people in the church who are prepared to go to extraordinary lengths to stop certain truths being said about them.'

Sister Veronica could feel the blood draining from her head. A dizziness took over and she shut her eyes.

'Are you all right, Sister?' Dominique's voice was full of concern. 'Have some of your coffee, the sugar in it will help you.'

Sister Veronica picked up her mug and drank. The room swam back into focus. She patted her pocket, trying to locate her emergency bag of custard creams.

'I've told you everything I know about Jamie's murder,' she said. 'As you can see, we still don't know who did it, whether it was someone in the church or outside.'

'True.' Dominique nodded. 'But what you do know is that the highest authorities are covering up his murder. Now why would they do that?'

They sat in silence for a minute.

'Who really was Jamie, Dominique?' Melissa asked. 'Do you have any more information about him that might help us?'

'I have his file here.' Dominique opened the plain file in front of her. 'We assign numbers to each priest's or nun's child's file, to help with confidentiality. Jamie was number 9453. The information we have about him is sparse, but I will tell you what we've got.' She shuffled some papers. 'It says here that he lived in Sidcup in Kent with his mother. He was attending art college near there until his suicide attempt a year ago. He had found out about his real father by going through his mother's personal documents. She'd brought him up believing that his real father had died in a car crash before Jamie was born – maybe his mother wanted this to be true, it's much more straightforward. But he found her diary from the year before his birth and it details her relationship with a priest. No name, just the fact she was in a relationship with a priest when she was studying theology at university. Jamie went to the church for help, he desperately needed to know who his father was. This is very common among priests' and nuns' children, as with most adults who discover their parentage is false, when they discover the lie they often develop an insatiable desire to know the truth of who their parent really is.' Melissa nodded. 'But the church didn't help him.' Dominique went on. 'He was at his wits' end when he received an anonymous letter a couple of months ago from a "well-wisher", with the name of the person who had orchestrated the secrecy and silencing of Jamie and his mother.'

'Who was it?' Sister Veronica asked sharply.

'I believe this man has been promoted since. But at the time of Jamie's birth, he was known as Father Henri Sabell.'

'Bishop Sabell.' Sister Veronica shook her head. 'No wonder Cardinal Moore wants this covered up.'

'Who's Bishop Sabell?' Melissa asked.

'Cardinal Moore's closest friend. They work together at the

Archbishop's House.' Sister Veronica frowned. 'So let me check I've got the facts right,' Sister Veronica said. 'Bishop Sabell orchestrated the silencing of Jamie.'

'Yes, he made Jamie's mother lie, he threatened her and said the bits of money she was being sent would stop if she ever spoke about the true identity of his father. She was scared of him,' Dominique said.

'But he wasn't actually Jamie's father?'

Dominique shook her head.

'Then who was?'

Dominique spread her hands wide.

'Nobody knows,' she said.

20

Cardinal Moore leaned back in his first-class seat, considering his next move as the plane accelerated down the runway. The priest, Mathers, was a disastrous failure, there was no doubt about that. He hadn't even contacted the Cardinal to say he couldn't find the old goat, Sister Veronica, sent no word, nothing. It was too bad. Unprofessional and unprincipled. Cardinal Moore ran a tight ship, and there was no room for this kind of inefficiency in it.

Of course, he'd left Henri in charge of tracing the errant nun. Damn her. Things had been going so smoothly up till then. But she couldn't be far, and she wouldn't have much money with her. The senseless woman wouldn't be able to get up to much anyway, she didn't have the intelligence. He cast his mind back to how she'd snorted and cried at the sight of the boy's body. Typical female, driven by emotions not logic. She'd probably fled because she didn't want to be ensconced in the closed convent in Cumbria. When he found her, he'd make sure she never left the damn place. A life-long contemplation session should bring her to heel.

Sister Julia had phoned just as he was about to leave for the airport. Apparently, the old nun, Sister Anastasia, had died in her sleep. Old age and a stroke. He'd given instructions for the funeral to be organised, and left them all to it. He had much greater things on his mind. He thought ahead to his meeting at the Vatican. There was something he badly needed his contact there to do that would help with the investigation, bring it to a satisfactory close. It was always tricky to raise such delicate matters within the inner circle there – a circle he was feeling increasingly part of, and quite rightly so. But considering the nature of his meeting in Rome, he was confident his contact wouldn't mind correcting a particular document for him, one of the only Vatican documents in existence about priests' children. Given Sister Veronica's Houdini-like tendencies it would be sensible to close down every possible loose end regarding Jamie Markham and his heritage at this stage.

He shut his eyes, a caustic grimace remaining etched on his face.

21

It was the cleaner, Tina Naylor, who discovered Father Mathers' body, the little trickle of blood from his mouth dried almost black, his eyes wide and staring.

When the police got there she was white-faced, dragging heavily on a cigarette, numbed with total shock.

'I ain't touched nothing,' she kept saying. 'The room was messed up like this when I got here. And him such a tidy man. I just came in like usual and there he was on the floor. I mean, who would kill a priest?'

She had to stay there while the police took her witness statement, and the forensic team came in and combed through the room, scraping unseen things from the floor, putting clothes in bags, photographing Father Mathers' body – and blood – from every angle.

'Burglary gone wrong?' she heard one of the officers ask the detective in charge.

'Mmm,' was the dubious reply.

22

'What did you call this?' Sister Veronica gave a polite smile as she peered down her nose at the list in front of her. Dominique's colleague, Victor Dubois, had arrived with some information for her. She was touched by how they'd both taken time off work that day to talk to her. A young girl who'd been introduced to her as Simone, and who had extremely long legs that sported the shortest shorts Sister Veronica had ever seen, sat typing at a laptop laconically, chewing gum.

'It's a list of supporters,' Victor said in broken English. 'Simone just printed it out, she is the best assistant anyone could have.' He smiled over at the girl and she winked back. 'People all over the world who we have got to know, who help our mission.'

'I see. And what exactly is your mission?' Sister Veronica asked.

Victor grinned. He had never met anyone quite like the old nun before.

'To help the children of priests and nuns. To support them, help them gain recognition from the Vatican, try and stop the shame, secrecy and stigma they are born into. As I believe Dominique has already told you, suicide attempts and mental illnesses are high among these people. As the son of a nun myself, who understands exactly what it feels like to be a living example of someone else's shame, it makes me angry that so many people have to live with this. It has to stop.' Victor had stopped smiling. Passion now lit his eyes. 'Do you know what it is like to live with a secret from the moment you're born, Sister? To have to lie, just so someone else's lie can be upheld? To not know who you really are, because your life has been twisted into a different story by well-meaning people?'

Sister Veronica nodded slowly.

'Yes, Victor,' she said quietly. 'Actually, I do.' The pain of remembering how she'd been silenced and had to live a lie ached through her, sharpening her devotion to finding out what had happened to Jamie and if he'd been silenced to help sustain a lie.

'Then you will understand why so many people feel so strongly about this,' he said. 'I am a Catholic, Sister, and I love my church. I would do anything for it. But these lies, this mistreatment of children and adults in the name of God, when God has nothing to do with this human-made mess, has to stop. Many priests and nuns, and members of the Roman Catholic Church feel the same. They want to help us too. They want their church to be a place of openness and peace, not one of dishonesty, fraud and vice. I mean, have you read the papers this morning?' Sister Veronica shook her head. 'There was a front-page piece about the head of a Catholic Church racketeering syndicate arrested in Chile. His name is Father Joaquin Vasquez. The article said they suspect this group is run within the Catholic Church remit all over the world, they just haven't been able to prove any other links. It's absurd, these crimes are always getting reported but it seems to make no dent on the church, and it never cleans up its act at all. It's like it's invincible. You told us Cardinal Moore wants to have you moved to an obscure convent, Sister, to silence you. Does that not remind you of what happened to Sister Vincenza after she discovered the murdered body of Pope John Paul I in 1978? She was also silenced and moved far away. You see, there is a precedent here. They like to create a Mafia-style *omertà* disguised as protocol.'

Sister Veronica nodded sadly.

'Unlike the terrible crimes committed with clerical sexual abuse,' Victor went on, 'where often it is just the priest and his victim who know the truth, with children of priests and nuns lots of people know the truth. You cannot easily hide a woman's pregnant belly. There are so many people complicit in this cover-up it is unbelievable. But some of those people change their minds and come to us, saying they want to help. And that is what this list is, Sister. A register of all the names of people around the world who are helping us.'

Sister Veronica nodded, acknowledging and feeling his desire to make the church a better place, his ache for positive change. Good. She was glad people like Victor and Dominique were there, helping and supporting these children, young and old. It was life-affirming to see positivity and compassion amid the dark chaos of murder and intrigue. Roman Catholic Church racketeering? Whatever next. She made a mental note to remember that for her next book, if she ever got a chance to write again with all this bedlam.

Feeling rejuvenated by Victor's emotional speech, she scanned down the list of names. Each had a country attached to them; Sister Teresita – Philippines. Father Lopez – Mexico. Her keen eyes looked for British connections. She didn't recognise the first two, Father Barnes and Sister Ellen. But then a name caught her eye. She started in surprise.

'Bishop Christopher Hammett?' she said. 'The same one who works in the Archbishop's House as the Cardinal's secretary?'

'The one and only.' Dominique smiled as Melissa came in carefully carrying a tray of freshly-steaming mugs. 'He has been part of our cause for two years now. And understandably so. He is a father himself, you know. Of a lovely girl who lives in England with his partner. He is torn up inside from trying to be a good priest, a good father and a good partner. I worry about him.'

Sister Veronica's mouth was wide open.

'It's not often she's stuck for words.' Melissa grinned, placing a mug of tea in front of the nun.

'Bishop Hammett wants to help you, Sister. He called me very early this morning. From what he said I understand he has some vital information that will help you. He's on his way to Paris now.'

'Excellent.' Melissa spoke for Sister Veronica, who was still digesting this latest revelation. Bishop Hammett? The father of a child? A supporter of Children of the Blessed? This whirlwind of discovery was taking some very unexpected turns indeed. 'Hmm. It feels quite strange, this bishop turning up. Kind of ominous...'

23

B efore Cardinal Moore entered the restaurant, he made a phone call.

'Henri,' he said when a voice answered. 'You know the man we spoke of before I left? No not Mathers, the other one. Yes, that's right. Have him watched, will you? Just a gut instinct. Oh, and tell the press to rerun the piece about clerical celibacy never ending. One more thing, Henri, phone O'Hara. I had a jumbled voicemail from him, the man made no sense whatsoever.' There was a short pause. 'What do you mean something's happened?' There was a long pause. 'Mathers? Thank you for this most interesting information. Oh and Henri, the assessors will be back tomorrow, please make them feel welcome. God bless you too, Henri.'

He smoothed down his shirt, and strode confidently into the restaurant, Squisito. Half empty, this middle-of-the-road tourist destination was the perfect meeting place, he thought, satisfied. He saw his contact at once, and made his way towards him.

'How's the investigation going?' Archbishop Cancio, secretary of the Pontifical Council asked as he sat down.

'Very well,' Cardinal Moore answered, his eyes taking the contents of the menu in at one glance.

'I heard there might have been a little, how do you say, hiccup?' Archbishop Cancio smiled lazily, as if he'd just taken Cardinal Moore's king in a chess game.

Cardinal Moore smiled back.

'Good news travels fast, I see, Matteo. Yes, we had a minor inconvenience but the team I have working on this now don't make mistakes. I made an error, which I am now fixing.'

'Relax, Charles. I'm just teasing you, you should know me better by now.' Archbishop Cancio poured another glass of wine and passed it to him. 'I wanted to let you know that we've become aware of a little loose end of yours that floated over to the continent. Paris, to be precise. We are in the process of tidying it up for you.'

Cardinal Moore stared at him, understanding.

'Thank you, Matteo. I will of course return the favour, should I ever need to.'

'I know you will, I know you will.' Archbishop Cancio sipped his wine. 'Now, on to more important matters. As you know, the plan has unfolded in exactly the way we anticipated so far, and the next stage is starting soon. I've got some figures here for you.' He took a folded piece of paper from his jacket pocket and handed it to Cardinal Moore. 'Take a look.'

The Cardinal unfolded the paper. He allowed his eyebrows to ascend a fraction of an inch. 'This is impressive, Matteo. Over a billion. It's rising to levels even I hadn't predicted.' He began shredding the paper into tiny bits.

'Yes, my friend, it is. And it will continue to grow if we are wise and make the right decisions. Bishop Paulo Alfonsi from the Vatican Bank wants to talk to you and I this evening. A Sicilian by the name of Guglielmo Turatello will also attend. I said you would be there, si?'

'Of course.' The men raised their glasses and toasted each other. Everything was about money and power, although neither would be so crass as to say such a thing. But these concepts, when made into realities, were the only things that ever ultimately mattered. That was the game.

'Actually, Matteo, there is something I need to ask you, to do with the other business. For the investigation to end in a satisfactorily final way, I need to see a copy of *Nota relative alla prassi della Congregazione per il Clero a proposito dei chierici con prole*. There's something I need to confirm regarding clerics with children, and possibly have – ah –amended. Could you do that for me?'

Archbishop Cancio regarded his compatriot as he took another sip of wine. He gave another lazy smile.

'For you, Charles, I can make that happen.'

24

'Sister, look!' Melissa was gesturing towards a newspaper stand. Sister Veronica was gazing longingly at a waiter deftly placing steaming plates before two hungry tourists. There was a relaxed feel in the Parisian streets, she'd noticed, despite the numerous people sitting at bistro tables or ambling about. The mouth-watering smells from every corner were impossible to ignore, and her stomach was complaining loudly.

'What is it?' she called, edging closer to the nearest brasserie's menu, posted neatly behind a glass screen near the café's door.

'Just come and look!' There was an edge to Melissa's voice. Sighing, and deeply inhaling the garlicky fragrance of moules et frites, Sister Veronica made her way to the newspaper stand.

'Oh my–' She stopped. Her body felt hot with rushing blood.

'*Breaking News: Money-Laundering Priest Found Dead At Home In London,*' she read. '*Father Zachary St John Mathers, suspected of embezzling churchgoers' funds, has been found dead at his home in St Joseph's rectory in Soho. A post-mortem is being carried out to determine the cause of death. Police say their investigations are continuing. A spokesperson for the Roman Catholic Church, Bishop*

Sabell, has issued the following statement: "We are greatly saddened to hear of the death of Father Mathers, and shocked by the allegations against him. We will continue to help the police in their investigations in any way we can."'

Sister Veronica felt sick. Another death, so soon after Jamie's. True, she hadn't liked the man at all, and she wasn't going to pretend she had now he was dead. But money-laundering priest? Embezzling churchgoers' funds? Like a whirring machine, information clicked into place in her head. The meeting she'd overheard in the convent, Father Mathers saying he needed more time. Had the foolish man really been trying to defraud honest churchgoers? But wait, the Cardinal had also asked him to keep an eye on her, she was sure of it. The way she'd heard them whispering that day at the hostel when she'd sneaked up to search Jamie's room. Was Father Mathers' death entirely unrelated to Jamie's murder? In these dark and twisted times it was hard to even guess.

'Are you okay, Sister?' Melissa put her hand on Sister Veronica's shoulder. 'You've gone very white.'

'Yes, yes,' she muttered. 'Just a shock, that's all. Awful man, didn't like him a jot. But another death, what if it's somehow connected to Jamie?'

Melissa stared at the paper, reading through the article.

'Well,' she considered. 'The accusations of embezzlement against him point to his death possibly relating to that. Maybe he found out the papers had got hold of the story and took his own life? He came across as very arrogant sometimes, although I don't want to speak ill of the dead. He probably didn't want his reputation ruined. Or maybe someone he'd double-crossed wanted revenge?'

Sister Veronica sighed.

'Yes, you're right, I shouldn't jump to conclusions.' She shook her head, trying to clear it. 'Right. Let's put that man out of our minds for now. Bishop Hammett will be meeting us soon. With this new discovery about Father Mathers I can't help but feel our own safety is even more compromised now. I'm not sure meeting someone else from inside the church is a good idea, but there we go. It seems strange that the bishop is coming all this way to help us. I do hope this is not a trap.'

25

Cardinal Moore's face had a hard edge as he pushed through the crowds in front of the Vatican's Sistine Chapel. Why weren't these people moving out of the way for him? Surely it was obvious who he was; the red-and-white robes more than gave it away. That was the problem with today's Catholics, they had no respect.

Several tourists milled around in front of its façade, hardly bothering to admire the fifteenth-century construction of Pope Sixtus IV.

'Philistines,' the Cardinal muttered as he pressed past them and into the interior of the chapel. He savoured the majestic artistic assault on his senses, letting the Renaissance masterpieces consume his attention for a minute or two. Then he walked to the back, tapping a code into a pad attached to an unassuming door. His destination was the usual private office he met his associates and business partners in, located two floors below the Papal apartments.

As Cardinal Moore entered the meeting room, he saw three men sitting round the table. Matteo was already there.

'Ah, Your Eminence, welcome.' Bishop Paulo Alfonsi was

already on his feet, ushering the Cardinal towards an ornate chair. 'Please, sit, sit. Here's some water, and some wine. You know His Grace already, of course. Let me introduce our great friend Guglielmo Turatello, who travelled from Sicily to be with us today.'

Turatello's moustache moved as his jowly face smiled, his chubby cheeks giving him a cherub-like look.

The men conversed in low voices for a while, catching up on news and sharing information.

'Gentlemen,' Bishop Alfonsi's voice called the meeting to order, 'our scheme has gone well, as you all know. The new bonds from America are being trialled at the moment, if successful – and they will be – they will bring us a net profit of €900,000 each. Your Eminence' – he turned to the Cardinal – 'a sample of the bonds will arrive in the UK tomorrow, going straight into the Wessex Building Society into the account you provided for us under the name Damien Hepworth. Please alert your contact to this, and ask him to observe and relay information after the bonds arrive and are processed. This will be the fourth and final trial before the main body of the bonds are invested through our partners in banks around the world.'

Cardinal Moore inclined his head in acknowledgement.

'Guglielmo here has had the highest of, how shall we say, new bonds created for us.' Bishop Alfonsi looked indulgently at the Sicilian. 'We've been working together for many years. Never before did such a trusting partnership exist.'

Archbishop Cancio chuckled.

'Of course, in Chile, our partner – Father Joaquin Vasquez – was not so lucky. The story quite tickled me as I read the papers today,' he said. 'Racketeering, I believe, is the charge.'

Bishop Alfonsi glared at the Archbishop.

'With respect, I arranged for that to happen, Your Grace,' he said. 'I had some documents about Vasquez leaked to the

Chilean police, after I gained information that he was siphoning far more than his share off. Let it be a warning to our other partners around the world.'

Archbishop Cancio clapped his hands.

'Oh, very good, very good.' He laughed. 'You're a smart man. I knew there was a reason I put you in charge of this.'

As Bishop Alfonsi and Turatello fell into conversation about the bonds, Cardinal Moore leaned towards Archbishop Cancio.

'Have you managed to change what I asked on the document for clergy with children, my friend?' he murmured.

'Of course, Charles. I added the information you gave me this very afternoon.' Archbishop Cancio smiled languidly.

It was only because Cardinal Moore looked down at his watch at that moment, that he missed the look Bishop Alfonsi gave Archbishop Cancio, the nod he received in reply, and the small, knowing smile that then passed between them.

26

B ack out on the street again and blinking in the sun, their stomachs comfortably full, Sister Veronica and Melissa made their way to the front of the church of Notre Dame de Lorette. Standing in the shade in front of the huge stone pillars, Sister Veronica surveyed the busy urban landscape in front of her. Before Dominique and Victor had returned to their day jobs, the French woman had told them where to meet Bishop Hammett. He'd phoned just as they were leaving the office to say he was nearly there, and Simone had passed his message straight on.

Sister Veronica couldn't put her finger on exactly why she felt this, but she had an unshakeable conviction that they were being watched. It was the same feeling she'd had that day in Putney, when she was on her way to Melissa's apartment. Well, nothing had come of that, so she was sure she shouldn't worry too much about this. Yet...

'Urgh,' Melissa said, looking at her phone.

'Is there something wrong?' Sister Veronica asked.

'Oh, it's just my dick – my idiot ex-boyfriend.' Melissa

grimaced. 'I've just got a text from him. He says he's sorry for the way he spoke to me the other day. He wants us to try again.'

'And what do you want, dear?'

'God knows.' Melissa sighed. 'I think I want to be with someone who really loves me, and doesn't want to change me.'

'Well, hold out for that then, Melissa. Don't compromise, you're a wonderful person. Wait for someone who can truly see that.'

'Thank you, Sister.' Melissa shot her a grin, turning back to the crowds.

'Sister Veronica! And this must be Melissa?' Bishop Hammett strode towards them, his clean-shaven face breaking into a smile. 'How lovely to see you both.'

'Bishop Hammett.' Sister Veronica nodded, then introduced Melissa, who gazed at the man very coolly. She wondered whether the girl was having the same thoughts as her: how much could they trust this man? She gave an internal chuckle. From what Melissa had just said, it sounded like neither of them were very impressed with the men in their lives at the moment. Then she remembered Father Mathers, and the sick feeling returned.

'Shall we go somewhere more private to talk?' Bishop Hammett said, when the introductions and polite enquiries about travel had been made. 'There's so much we need to discuss.'

By the time they'd located a quiet space of grass down Rue de Châteaudun – Sister Veronica periodically checking over her shoulder – and settled down to talk, Bishop Hammett's smile had long since left, with well-creased worry lines dominating his face instead.

'Yes, it's true I have a daughter.' Bishop Hammett bowed his head. 'God forgive me, I am weak when it comes to the flesh. But I love the Catholic Church and want to continue in my ministry.

I know I can help people, but I love my daughter and my partner, Anna, too. This conflict tortures me every day.'

Sister Veronica's stiff posture relaxed as tears oozed out of the bishop's eyes.

'Love, as St Paul said, is indeed the most important thing, Your Grace. It is very heart-warming to hear how much you love your child and partner and also the church.' She smiled at him. 'I am beginning to think that clerical celibacy is a myth, and that I am the only member of the cloth who is not a parent.' Sister Veronica allowed herself a small chuckle. 'The problem driving the whole terrible business of Jamie's life and murder, is the *absence* of love. When Jamie and other children of the ordained attempt suicide, I believe this is caused by their internalisation of shame. This is a lack of love not only from their fathers, and sometimes their mothers, but from the church – who often don't help them from what I've been told – from society, who read about scandalous naughty priest fathers being disgraced in newspapers, from friends and families who have helped silence the child by perpetrating the lie about their parentage. And this is all done to protect the *good*' – she spat the word – 'name of the church. Do you see? These children, young and old, not only have to deal with all these lies and rejection, but come to terms that this is done in the name of God. It's all right if their fathers and mothers reject them, because it's what God wants. Well, I'll tell you something, my God does NOT want children to be treated like this.' Sister Veronica had fire in her eyes.

Bishop Hammett was nodding slowly, his tears drying on his cheeks. Melissa wrote feverishly in her notepad.

'And I'll tell you something else,' Sister Veronica went on, 'the ultimate antithesis of love was shown to Jamie; someone had the audacity to take away his most precious thing – his life. So you see, Your Grace' – Sister Veronica leant her reddening face towards his – 'I'm glad to hear of your love for your child and for the church. If more people were like you, we wouldn't be in this bloody mess.'

She sat back, breathing deeply.

'Thank you, Sister.' Bishop Hammett took her hands in his trembling ones. 'Thank you. It has done me the world of good to hear your words. And I agree with every single one of them. The note warning you about Cardinal Moore was from me, by the way, because I knew you were working to bring a ray of light to a dark situation, and within the confines of some corrupt people, and I wanted to help you.'

'You?' Sister Veronica eyed him, wondering if she could trust what he was saying. It was so hard to tell who was friend or foe these days.

'Yes. I couldn't have revealed my identity to you at the time as I was still surrounded by those in the thrall of very immoral power, and I didn't know who I could trust. Although many of the people I work with are wonderful, several are not. So apologies for the cryptic message but it was the best I could do at the time.'

Sister Veronica sat surveying him in silence for a moment or two, then her shoulders relaxed and she gave a small smile.

'But what I don't understand' – Melissa looked up, laying down her pen – 'is why Cardinal Moore wanted to keep Jamie's death so secret. Why the big fuss? Why is he trying to send Sister Veronica away? Why not just let the police deal with it, it would be much easier for him.'

'Ah, now that I may be able to help answer.' Bishop Hammett's face was regaining colour, his voice now more self-assured. He reached into the inside pocket of his jacket and retrieved a folded piece of paper. 'Before I show you this, let me explain something. As you will no doubt have heard from the hard-working Dominique and Victor, who have done so much for children of priests, nuns and their parents, there is a growing band of supporters of their work around the world.'

Sister Veronica and Melissa nodded.

'Many are like me, they love their ministry but they see the mandatory clerical celibacy discipline as outdated and irrelevant in our modern times.'

Sister Veronica snorted at the word 'modern'.

'These supporters come in all shapes and forms, some are lay people, some priests and nuns, some bishops like me, and some belong to the higher ranks in the church such as archbishops. We even have one or two cardinals. And' – he paused – 'we have contacts in the Vatican itself. I spoke to one on the way here, and he is keen to help you. His contact details are on this paper.'

He passed it to Sister Veronica. She opened it and read.

'But,' Bishop Hammett went on, 'the problem is that there is much evil in the church, as well as goodness. And unfortunately, the epicentre of this is in the Vatican. There are several key players there who appear on the outside to be the most traditional members of the clergy, the best rule-keepers, the dogma enthusiasts. But underneath, they are the biggest crooks and liars. I'm reliably informed that they have their fingers in an unbelievable amount of unsavoury pies. And many of them count Cardinal Moore as a very close friend. The way they have information at their fingertips is unbelievable. I have to warn you, Sister, that someone at the Vatican had already heard you were in France. The Catholic Church's upper echelons around the world are like a series of nosy villages. News gets passed from one to the other before the subject of the news has even got out of bed in the morning.'

'What?' Melissa said. 'Are you serious?'

'Deadly serious,' Bishop Hammett said. 'Sister Veronica, I cannot emphasise enough how fragile your safety is now. I'm sorry to say this, but you must be so careful. Trust lightly, and keep looking over your shoulder, as I saw you doing earlier. By finding Jamie's body, witnessing the Cardinal's response to it, being daring enough not to submit to His Eminence's instructions of being silenced far away in a closed order, and finally jumping ship to mount your own investigation – which, by the way, those at the Archbishop's House are convinced you're doing – you have come up as a glaring hazard light on the Vatican's radar, that some more corrupt inhabitants there believe must be eliminated. But there are very good people in power too, and the contact I've given you is one of them.'

Sister Veronica stared at him.

'Have you heard about Father Mathers?' she asked.

Bishop Hammett nodded his head.

'It's a terrible affair, the whole thing. I never took to the man myself, he was so full of himself. But to die before one's time is always a tragedy. We must commend his soul to the Lord. And also poor Sister Anastasia's soul, of course.'

'Sister Anastasia?' Melissa asked, as Sister Veronica raised her eyebrows. 'Has she passed away too?'

'Oh, haven't you heard? No, of course, you've been busy travelling. Yes, the poor thing passed away in her sleep yesterday evening.'

Sister Veronica gazed into space, memories of Sister Anastasia's painful words to her assaulting her mind, the impact of her death awful and deep.

'In my opinion,' she said. 'Either there is an unusual spate of unrelated deaths going on within the Diocese of Westminster, or there may be a serial killer on the loose. And that frightens me to the core of my being.'

'But,' Melissa said, 'Sister Anastasia was very old, wasn't she? You said she'd had a stroke, it sounds like she died from natural causes.'

'What caused the final stroke, if that's what it was?' Sister Veronica retorted bluntly. 'When I went to visit her, she whispered in my ear that she knew what happened. She said the word "murder". I am fully convinced that Sister Anastasia was in the convent garden at the time of Jamie's murder, and heard more than she could say. Don't forget, since going blind her hearing had sharpened. If only she could have told me more when I saw her that day. If only I'd known the right questions to ask her.'

'I have to agree with you, Sister, there are sinister goings-on in Westminster at the moment.' Bishop Hammett's face was grave. 'I'm glad to be away from it. But like I said, be careful wherever you are these days.'

Sister Veronica frowned at him.

'So what on earth are we going to do?' she asked.

'Dominique told me that the lovely Simone at their office has arranged for us to stay in a safe house near Paris tonight. It is at a convent full of sympathisers for the cause. Tomorrow we travel to Rome, and meet the contact. He will know what to do, he will help you.'

Melissa caught Sister Veronica's eye.

'Looks like we better get back to Sean's and pack our stuff up then.'

27

'Melissa, write something down for me, please, would you?' Sister Veronica stared straight ahead, thinking hard. They were cruising along in the back seat of a cab, Bishop Hammett sitting next to the driver in the front. Unlike most of the taxi drivers Sister Veronica had spotted out of her window, their driver did not seem to have a death wish, and drove calmly and staidly, which pleased her immensely. Wiping crumbs from her shirt, the last remnants from the delicious baguette Simone had provided for the journey, she turned to look at her friend.

'Yup.' Melissa fumbled for her pad and pen. 'What do you want me to write?'

'I just want you to write down everything we know about Jamie and his death.' Sister Veronica's eyes winced. 'I've been trying to hold all the information in my brain, and sort it out into some kind of order, but all that's doing is giving me a headache.' She thumped the seat with her hand. 'And I feel so frustrated, Melissa. We've travelled far, but in reality it feels like we're going round in circles. We get this bit of information, that bit of information, but what do we really know? Are we actually any closer to the truth, or are we on a wild goose chase?'

'Good idea, Sister,' Melissa said soothingly. She was getting used to the nun's passionate outbreaks, that were so different to her otherwise headmistressy attitude. 'Ready when you are.'

'Good. Right. First, can you write down that on the day Jamie was murdered, I found his body at about half past three. He was last seen alive at breakfast time that day. The Cardinal immediately ordered his murder to remain secret, and you saw the assessors enter the hostel that evening. I found Jamie's diary and discovered that he was going to disclose something to me.'

Melissa dutifully scribbled away.

'The next day,' Sister Veronica went on, 'I discovered the Cardinal wanted to send me away, supposedly to keep me from talking about Jamie's death. It seems Sister Anastasia heard the murder, collapsed, and was taken into hospital. She has now died so I am unable to get any more information from the poor soul, may she rest in peace.' Sister Veronica bowed her head for a moment, while Melissa continued to write.

'Father Mathers, who was party to the Cardinal's wishes about me being sent away, is now also dead. Presumed murdered.' Sister Veronica's eyed flashed with darkness. 'Could Cardinal Moore be Jamie's father? Is that why he is so eager to cover this up? He is an ambitious man, there's no doubt about that. A scandal that proved his lack of celibacy would certainly end his plans to progress further in the church. But I find the thought that a father could do anything so awful to his child too abominable to entertain.' Or do I? she asked herself, remembering her own circumstances.

'We know from Bishop Hammett, and the Children of the Blessed team, just how rife the lack of celibacy is in the church. We know there are supporters, who want priests and nuns to be good parents while carrying on in their ministry, and we know there are the dogma enthusiasts who will seemingly do anything to keep the myth of clerical celibacy alive. Are you getting all this?'

'Yep,' Melissa said. 'Anything else?'

'We also now know, if Bishop Hammett is to be trusted – which I believe he is, after all, what choice do we have, and after all, he did help me by sending that note about Cardinal Moore's intentions – that there are both supporters and enemies in the highest echelons of the Vatican. And that there is much evil corruption going on too, just look at these charges of racketeering. Anything less holy, I really can't imagine.' Sister Veronica shook her head.

'So it seems,' she went on, 'that we are fighting against a big wall of silence. They want to cover up Jamie's murder and my witnessing of the body, yet we want to bring this out into the open, and for justice to be served. For all priests' and nuns' children,' she added.

Sister Veronica gave a sideways look to the nun who held the convent door open for them. The woman had quietly introduced herself as Sister Gabrielle. Previously, Sister Veronica would have automatically trusted her, but now she was wondering what her French sister knew. What church secrets was she privy to? Since Jamie's murder her world had been turned upside down. She felt like she no longer knew anyone anymore. A person who had the title priest or nun was no longer an instinctively safe presence, if anything, she felt less secure in the presence of new clergy. Nevertheless, she entered the convent respectfully and went through the appropriate greetings.

Sister Gabrielle emanated peace and reserve, and she felt

her tight mental vigilance relax a little. The sister showed them around – the small convent had originally been a medieval house. Its plain stone walls, clockwise circular staircases, large wooden dining table, open hearth, and surrounding rolling countryside had an instant soothing effect after the chaotic events of the previous few days. An older nun was seated in a rocking chair near the hearth. A younger one was reading at the dining table. Outside, some sisters gardened in friendly solitude.

'Le dîner est à sept heures et demie,' Sister Gabrielle said, depositing them outside their rooms before turning away.

'The dinner is at half past seven. Thank you, Sister,' Sister Veronica called after her. 'I'm going to have a quick nap, Melissa. This heat is exhausting.'

'Okay, no problem, I'll knock for you just before dinner.'

Sister Veronica had only intended to shut her eyes for a few minutes, but as soon as she lay down on the surprisingly comfy narrow bed, she sank into a deep sleep. So it was with disorientation that she forced her eyes open when she felt Melissa shaking her.

'Sister, Sister, it's time for dinner. Blimey, you were out cold then, I've been shaking your shoulder for a good two minutes.'

All the other sisters, and Bishop Hammett, were seated on the long wooden benches when they finally arrived downstairs; Sister Veronica's hair sticking out at wild angles.

The fish was a little dry, but it didn't matter, it was food. She wolfed it down, and accepted a second glass of wine from the old nun sitting opposite her.

A great wooziness overtook her mind. She tried to reach for her glass of water, and knocked over the pepper pot. A stabbing pain shot through her stomach and she groaned, collapsing forward on to the table.

'Sister, what's wrong?' Melissa rose in alarm.

Sister Veronica could hear panicked voices in the background. Her head span, her pulse raced, and she needed to vomit. She tried to say something but her muscles wouldn't work. There was something wrong.

28

'What, Sister? What did you say?' Bishop Hammett was kneeling down next to her head.

'I-I-I–' Sister Veronica slurred.

'Yes?' he asked. 'Try again, Sister.'

'Phone an ambulance,' Melissa said, taking charge. 'Bishop Hammett, please help me get Sister Veronica to a bed, she needs to lie down.' She wedged a shoulder under the nun's.

'The guest room is next door,' Sister Gabrielle said. 'Take her there.'

The old nun who had served Sister Veronica the wine during dinner watched, her face severe. Then she rose slowly and exited the room.

Sister Veronica's world was fuzzy, incoherent. Phrases from the people around her faded in and out.

'Have you called an ambulance yet?'

'Hold her, she nearly fell off the bed then.'

The room was moving now, a kaleidoscope of distortions. Was she on a bed, or maybe a raft? Waves of nausea rose and fell like the tide.

'Please wait,' Sister Gabrielle's voice floated above her. 'I think our oldest resident, Sister Noelle–'

'No, I will not bloody wait!' Melissa's voice was shrill. 'My friend has collapsed and you are all standing around like idiots just watching her. Phone the fucking ambulance NOW, Sister. Can't you see her life is in danger? For God's sake. My phone's in my room, can someone get it?'

A blackness swamped Sister Veronica, a welcome relief. But then fear. She was dying, she knew it now.

'Please.' A thin voice, a thick French accent. 'Let me give her this. I have seen these symptoms before, I think I know what has happened.'

'What?'

'She has been poisoned.'

Sounds of bottles being unscrewed, mixtures decanted and stirred.

'Charcoal is an antidote to many poisons,' Sister Gabrielle's voice said. 'Sister Noelle trained to be a doctor before receiving her calling from God. A few years ago she administered activated charcoal to a dog who ate poisoned meat and the dog survived.'

'Sister Veronica is not a bloody dog.' Bishop Hammett's voice. 'Have you all gone mad?'

'Wait.' Melissa's voice. 'Look.'

Sister Veronica felt a tube-like object being shoved into her mouth and squeezed. Rough, old fingers pinched her lips tightly shut. She struggled, choking, a mixture of something sliding down her throat.

Time stayed still for a minute.

Then a tidal wave of nausea ripped through her body, and she was sitting up before the huge stream of sickness left her mouth, soaking the white sheet.

She opened her eyes and saw Sister Gabrielle hurrying forward with a bowl.

'You poor thing.' Melissa, her make-up smudged, her eyes red-rimmed, stood next to the bed. Sister Veronica sank back, her limbs heavy with exhaustion.

The old nun, Sister Noelle, stood at the foot of the bed, observing.

Sister Veronica smiled weakly.

'Thank you.'

Sister Noelle nodded.

'You are okay now, I think.'

'Yes, you are getting some colour back.' Bishop Hammett leaned forward, concerned. Melissa stepped sideways away from him.

'Poison,' she said. She turned towards him. 'And I thought we were surrounded by friends here. Perhaps I was wrong.'

Bishop Hammett stared back at Melissa.

'You can't really think I–'

'I don't know what to think.' Melissa's voice was brisk, businesslike. 'Shouldn't we call the police? Someone here has just made a murder attempt.'

'No.' Bishop Hammett shook his head. Melissa raised her eyebrows. 'The police would inform too many others in the church. It seems our whereabouts are already known by those who wish Sister harm, but if the authorities got involved they may well insist that Sister Veronica goes to hospital, and from there they may transfer her back to the Convent of the Christian Heart, where she'll be a sitting target for anyone who wants to harm her.'

Melissa folded her arms.

'Look, someone just tried to kill Sister Veronica, we know that now.' Bishop Hammett ran both hands through his hair. 'If she'd had an allergic reaction to something in the food, the charcoal antidote wouldn't have worked. It would have only worked with poison. And no, Melissa, it wasn't me. I can see what you're thinking but I can assure you, on my life and the life of my child, that it wasn't me.'

Melissa shook her head, then bent down to stroke hair away from her friend's eyes.

'Well, it's too late to move anywhere tonight. I'll sleep in your room with you tonight, Sister. Then we can make plans tomorrow morning. Try and get some rest now.'

Sister Veronica gave the faintest of nods. Her eyes closed, the weight of relief at surviving near death and the exhaustion of it all causing her to fall into deep sleep.

Bishop Hammett shook his head, turned, and strode out of the room, his face unreadable.

29

Melissa massaged the suds into her aching head. Last night the floor had been hard, the blanket not thick enough, and she'd had a feeling she should stay 'on guard' in case anyone arrived to try and inflict harm on Sister Veronica again, so sleep had been fairly non-existent. She felt uneasy being in the convent, yet she had no option but to stay. Her friend needed her, and she wasn't about to let the old lady down. She didn't usually bond with people so quickly, didn't give a stuff about what they thought of her, but with Sister Veronica it was different. The old girl was special; her opinion mattered. She turned on the water again and let the surprisingly strong cascade drench her. If only it could really wash all her troubles away.

Drying herself and dressing, she tried to think of the bigger picture, but none came. What the fuck were they going to do? At times this journey had felt like an adventure, but now it was a living nightmare. She felt sorry she'd implied that Bishop Hammett was the perpetrator, but at the same time who else could it be? How much trust could she put in his words? Her gut instinct told her – what did her gut instinct tell her? That she had none when it came to trusting men in general. She'd actually warmed to Bishop Hammett, he had a depth of character to him that most men she knew didn't have, at least that was how he had seemed at first. But her defensive walls had come up as soon as he was under her suspicion. Why did she feel so disappointed about this? Get a grip, Melissa, she told herself. Seriously.

Stepping into the kitchen, the colder air was a relief, the stone walls soothing, the cool natural stone welcome.

Sister Veronica smiled at her. She was sitting at the wooden table, a cup of steaming coffee and a folded newspaper in front of her. The comforting smell of toast reached her nose, and suddenly she was hungry, ravenous, in fact.

'Please. Eat.' Sister Gabrielle put a freshly-buttered round of toast on the table, wiping her hands on her apron. 'Sister Veronica looks well this morning, yes?'

'Yes, thank God.' Melissa slid onto the bench. 'Thank you, Sister, this is just what I need. Where is Bishop Hammett?'

'Walking in the gardens. I fear he has a tortured soul, poor man.' Sister Veronica sighed, glancing towards the window.

'I don't think I made his soul feel any better yesterday,' Melissa said, taking a bite, savouring the thick buttery taste. 'It's just that everything seemed to go out of control as soon as he arrived. I just didn't want him to hurt you, Sister. But maybe I was wrong.'

'Sister Gabrielle has some information you need to hear, my dear.' Sister Veronica smiled at Melissa then nodded at the French nun.

'Early this morning, I had a phone call from our contact in the Vatican,' Sister Gabrielle said, coming closer. 'He said he has heard the name Simone mentioned in certain circles recently, and felt this might be someone in the pay of those who hold the power, someone of interest to us. Sister Veronica tells me this name means something to you all.'

'Oh God, the leggy blonde secretary from Children of the Blessed.' Melissa placed her toast down.

'Indeed,' Sister Veronica murmured.

'And I hear she made you all something to eat yesterday?' Sister Gabrielle said.

'Those baguettes.' Melissa closed her eyes, her hands going to her head. 'Why didn't I think of that? She asked us what fillings we wanted and wrote our names on the packets. So Bishop Hammett isn't–' She looked down, shaking her head slightly. Shit. Apologising was so cringingly difficult; you never knew how the other person would react, whether they would be cool about it or make you feel worse. Now listen, shut up and grow a pair, Melissa told herself. If you get things wrong, you can be woman enough to put them right. End of.

'What's that picture on the newspaper, Sister?' Melissa craned to see, eager for a temporary distraction. A dour-faced man wearing a dog collar stared back.

'Ah yes, yet another sad story, I fear.' Sister Veronica sighed. 'Sister Gabrielle, would you translate for us?'

'Of course.' The nun picked up the paper. 'Let's see. Yes. It says, "Police arrest paedophile priest in Lyon. Archbishop Raphael Leclercq is accused of abusing girls over a fourteen-year period, during the time he was the diocesan priest in Lyon. Two of the girls claim to have given birth to Archbishop Leclercq's children at the ages of sixteen and seventeen. He denies these allegations. Police say DNA results will confirm whether or not Archbishop Leclercq is the father."'

'It never ends, does it?' Melissa said, picking up her toast again.

'What never ends?' Bishop Hammett walked through the door, his lined face more strained than ever. He was not looking much like a priest, Melissa noticed, with no dog collar, a navy chunkily-knitted sweater and beige cargo trousers. It must be windy today, she thought, as his longish hair was swept back chaotically.

'Revelations about priestly transgressions and misconduct.' Sister Veronica smiled sadly at him, then motioned towards the newspaper.

'Yeah, I agree. But some of us get a bad rap because of the bastards who can't behave. We are not all like that, despite current prejudice.' He shot a meaningful look at Melissa.

'Ouch. But fair enough, under the circumstances. Look, I'm really sorry about yesterday.' She sighed. 'I shouldn't have jumped to conclusions and blamed you, it wasn't fair. I was really scared and everything seemed to be going out of control. I-I find it hard to trust men.' She felt hot pink flush through her cheeks. 'Maybe that was partly why I put the blame on you so quickly, Bishop Hammett. Habit.'

Bishop Hammett's face softened.

'Apology accepted. And can you please all call me Chris? Bishop Hammett sounds frighteningly formal. Well, if I'm off the hook, who poisoned you, Sister Veronica?'

Over tea and more toast, they filled him in on the news about Simone.

Sister Gabrielle excused herself and serenely exited the room saying she needed to prepare the chapel for prayers.

Sister Veronica took a draught of her now lukewarm coffee and stared straight ahead, not paying attention to the chatter of the other two. Well, this was a turn of events, and no mistake. She was enough of a danger to the powers that be for them to want to make her disappear for good, this much was now glaringly clear. But for the church leadership was this really all about priests' children? About hiding Jamie's murder? Killing someone was in itself evil enough for a murderer or murderers to go to great lengths to cover their tracks, especially when such a crime would contrast in the starkest terms with the apparent high morality of their profession. Priests were the messengers of Jesus Christ on earth, weren't they? She chuckled darkly. Not some of them. Oh no, some came from the opposite place, the fiery depths, she knew that now. But what was all this about fake bonds? And criminal global rings within the Catholic Church? It sounded too far-fetched and ludicrous to be true. But as the memory of poor Jamie's battered body flashed into her mind yet again, suddenly fake bonds didn't seem so preposterous. Now anything seemed possible within the dark recesses of secrecy and corruption that had enveloped her life. And someone – possibly Simone, working for who? – had just tried to poison her. How had life come to this? No time for questions now, Veronica, she told herself sternly. They can come later.

What she needed was some peace and contemplation. The others didn't look up from their deep conversation as she quietly left the room. Just the act of entering the chapel broke through the silent darkness in her head. She found a pew, the residual pain in her stomach left over from yesterday forcing her to sit rather than kneel. A calmness and joy washed through her as she closed her eyes and bowed her head in prayer.

Listen, God, source of everything, love, or whatever or whoever you are, she thought. You can see what's going on here, and I can't, not yet. You can see what some people are doing in your name, the crimes they are committing, the levels of subterfuge, criminality and corruption they are prepared to go to for their own ends. Now, listen. I'm here, doing my absolute best to find justice for poor Jamie. But God, please, you have to help us now. Point us in the right direction at least. Because, quite frankly, I could do with your help.

Sister Gabrielle's words, that her contact in the Vatican had told her about Simone, floated into her mind. Was it the same contact held by Children of the Blessed? If the Vatican was the powerhouse, if it was there that decisions were made to poison, hide, make invisible, and silence people, then it was there that answers were to be found, the only place they were to be found. They must find a way to enter the lion's den. This wasn't just Jamie's fight, it was hers too, as well as many other priests' children around the world. Going to the Vatican was their best – only – chance of finding out who thought it acceptable to murder in order to publicly uphold a vow of celibacy that had in reality been broken. Who thought taking a life was worth this deception, this unspeakable lie and hypocrisy. She said a silent prayer of thanks for the newly boiling blood coursing through her veins.

30

Cardinal Moore, having been to morning prayers in the sumptuous Sistine Chapel, now tapped a pen repeatedly against the polished wooden desktop before him, his half full glass of expensive port glistening. An unfamiliar uneasiness was bothering him.

He had been hoping and expecting someone to bring word overnight that the latest stage of the plan back in London was unfolding smoothly, like it always had done before. But instead, Matteo, his striking blue eyes glinting angrily in a way that had made Cardinal Moore both enthralled and concerned, had arrived at 4am with the news that the interfering old nun was still active in France. Rather than a sudden bout of ill health ending her plight, it seemed – if their Parisian contact was to be believed – that she and her amassed entourage were now firmly dug in, in a miserable little convent outside Paris. Honestly, was the woman indestructible? But right now, she wasn't his main source of disquiet.

The tips of his fingers touched gently as he brought his hands together under his chin. He needed news from London. Something wasn't right, he could feel it. By his calculations, news should have reached him by now. The silence was disturbing. His hand reached out for the phone, then hesitated, and he drew it back. Then he reached out again, this time lifting the receiver and dialling the switchboard.

The switchboard was charming and outdated, both comforting and irritating. In a very plainly furnished room on the second floor of the Vatican, a batch of multilingual nuns sat in grey habits answering incoming calls in calm tones. 'Pronto, Vaticano.' (Hello, Vatican.) They reiterated the phrase from 8am until 8pm every day, dealing with more than half a million enquiries every year. They hailed all comers with the same gentle serenity and tackled the intricacy of the bureaucracy in the Roman Catholic Church with grace. It was not the dedication of these nuns that Cardinal Moore questioned, they were quite rightly doing their female duty of service, more the fact that he was convinced that there was a real chance that some of them may have more than one master. Since he could not use his mobile phone as a signal was so intermittent here, he had no choice but to ask to be given a line. He would have to be very careful about what he said.

A male voice answered on the second ring.

'Having a lot of problems with mobile signals here at the moment, which is why I'm calling you through the switchboard.' The Cardinal spoke quickly, placing heavier emphasis on the last word. There was a moment's hesitation before the voice said:

'I have heard, just now, that there's been a problem with the – er – tea.'

'I see, is this a temporary problem, or is the tea still being made?'

'I'm not sure.'

'I see,' Cardinal Moore said again. 'Keep me informed.'

'I will.'

Cardinal Moore picked up the pen and tapped with renewed frenzy. And he'd been feeling so renewed, so full of zest after midnight prayers. It made the crash back to life's worries even more tiresome. Last night, just being in the same room as Cardinal Federico Pisano, the Vatican's Secretary of State and second in command to the Pope, had been thrilling. Matteo and Bishop Alfonsi had been there too, but Guglielmo, through tacit understanding, knew he was not permitted. Power dripped from Pisano, the man had such command. And Cardinal Moore knew he understood how things worked. He just got it, in a way the current Pope didn't.

'Look around,' Cardinal Pisano had said to the packed chapel. 'You are the chosen ones, you are special. Princes among men. God needs you and wants you to maintain the natural order of things.'

There had been murmurs of agreement.

'It is a hard job for us today, my friends,' Cardinal Pisano had said. 'So many well-meaning people disrupt this order, they do not understand that their misplaced notions of equality actually bring chaos, and lead our world towards disaster. But we understand, don't we?'

A chorus of assent, and nodding of heads.

'We understand that God has chosen us to lead, to bring humanity to him, and to rid the world of sin. And what do we need to do to ensure this happens? We need to lead, we need to network with the most powerful in this world to safeguard our continuity, because for continuity we need resources, and above all we need to protect the holy name of the Roman Catholic Church, whatever the cost.'

We *are* special, Cardinal Moore mused, as his thoughts caused some zest to return. We *are* the chosen ones. Why is that so hard for people to understand? It's what God wants. It's the natural order of things. People need leaders, otherwise they go off track and ruin things. They need to learn to behave, and follow rules set for their own good. People are like sheep, and I am their shepherd. Sometimes a damaged animal needs to be put down, of course, before it causes infection among the flock. And on occasion, damaged people need the same treatment, before they infect the masses with their pestilent freethinking and unnecessary problem-causing. The sooner that interfering old nun is caught, the sooner the system can go back to running smoothly, as it ought to.

31

'Right,' Sister Veronica said, walking back into the kitchen. The other two were still there, heads together, lost in deep conversation. 'Now, I have been thinking,' she said loudly. 'And I have come to the conclusion that the only way we can progress with this any further, is by going to the Vatican.'

'I've been thinking the same.' Melissa's head snapped up, and Sister Veronica's sharp eyes noticed a slight flush on her cheeks.

Bishop Hammett cleared his throat and shifted position.

'Sister, if you are feeling well enough, I suggest that we leave today.'

'That suits me,' Sister Veronica said. 'My throat is feeling much better, I think Sister Noelle's potion of honey and vinegar has really soothed it. But what is the best way to get there? Before yesterday I would have felt stupid saying this, but presumably airports and train stations would be the worst places to go at the moment, in case Vatican watchers are monitoring them.'

'Hire car,' Melissa said immediately. 'We can book it under

an assumed name and we can make sure we are not being followed, do you think, Chris – Bishop Hammett?'

'Yes,' Bishop Hammett nodded in agreement. 'That would give us the most amount of freedom.'

Sister Veronica nodded slowly.

'Let's go and pack,' Melissa said. 'I'll ask Sister Gabrielle to book us a taxi. I'm ready to leave this place. There was me thinking convent life was calm and peaceful but on discovery it actually turns out to be fraught with danger. I don't think it's for me after all.' She laughed.

'No, I have no doubt that it is not,' Chris murmured, holding out his hand as Melissa swung her long legs out from under the table.

Within the hour they were ready to go. Sister Gabrielle and Sister Noelle waved them off, and as the taxi pulled away Sister Veronica felt a pang of longing, not knowing when, if ever, she might find herself safely within convent walls again. Since her poisoning she had experienced a deep peace and tranquillity within the French convent's walls that she had not felt for a long time. And finding peace of mind was *so* important, especially when the world around her had gone mad.

They spoke little on the way to the hire car company, each one of them lost in their own thoughts. It had been Melissa's idea to get a taxi there, rather than ring for one. It was best to do everything they could to avoid detection, she'd said. Standing in the queue for the car, she heard the bishop say behind her, 'Aren't those uncomfortable?'

'My piercings? Nah, I'm so used to them, do you like them?'

'Well, actually, they rather suit you.'

Sister Veronica thought hard. She would, she felt, have to have a quiet word with Melissa very soon. Or maybe she should just leave the journey of love, or whatever this was, to run its course. After all, what business was it of hers? She had more important things to worry about.

They hired a car. As he climbed into the driver's seat, the bishop assured the other two that he was used to long journeys, and that he had driven this exact route three years previously.

'I've been to Rome four times, actually.' He turned to Melissa, who was folding herself into the front passenger seat of the Fiat Cinquecento. Sister Veronica busily spread her skirt out over the back seat. 'When I'm driving in Rome I have to measure my success incrementally. The best drivers in Italy understand that they create a moving work of art – a harmonious masterpiece like the ceiling of the Sistine Chapel – with other vehicles by pressing together; the unspoken law is that the most antagonistic driver will always be awarded first place on the road. Sometimes I like to be that driver.'

Melissa giggled and tucked a strand of pink-and-blonde hair behind her ear.

And this, Sister Veronica thought wearily as she observed the chemistry between them blossom, is why there are so many priests' children in the world. Because priests are humans, like everybody else. They fall in love, they feel attraction, they cannot tell how they will feel from one day to the next. Oh yes, I'll take a vow of celibacy, and on this precise day I one hundred per cent mean it. Fast forward to sometime in the future, when loneliness has set in, or that unexpected chemical fusion has spontaneously taken place with another person, and suddenly celibacy – or perhaps chastity – is not such a straightforward concept to adhere to. So who is in the wrong, the church for having that mandatory vow, or the priests for breaking it?

She sat, lost in thought for a moment, a seething rage growing in her as dusk turned to night outside.

It's a systemic problem at the core of the Catholic Church, she decided. If it were collectively possible to be celibate forever, there wouldn't be thousands of priests' children in existence, being hidden and silenced. Are all their fathers really the badly behaved black sheep of Catholicism, as they are made out to be in the press? Or is the mandatory clerical celibacy vow simply inhumane and untenable, and the solution to the unwanted children even more brutal? Welcome to the world, little baby. Your birthright is to be the living embodiment of the shame of your priest father. And a massive institution, the Catholic Church, is encouraging him to put his public – deceptive – image as a celibate priest over and above your mental and emotional health, and your right to a loving father. Hey, one day you might even be killed so that the church can continue its hypocritical public stance on celibacy. Because, after all, that is more important than your life. Now sleep well, and try not to feel too bad about yourself as you grow up. Oh, you've developed identity problems? Well never mind, it's just because the leadership of one of the five main global religions has discarded you as collateral damage. Haven't you worked out by now that their need for continued control and power is more important than you?

Her fingernails dug deeper and deeper into the palms of her hands until they broke the skin. Brooding thoughts continued to reel through her head and they were on the toll road to Italy before she fell into a fitful sleep.

She awoke to the sound of Bishop Hammett's hand on the horn. It was blending with hooters being deployed from all around, creating such a cacophony of noise that Sister Veronica sat bolt upright wondering if the Apocalypse had arrived. Bright sunlight gleamed through the windows, and she could see azure sky behind it. As a taxi got close to them, its wing mirror pinged off theirs.

'The thing is,' Bishop Hammett was saying, 'one can never hesitate here, the phrase "he who hesitates is lost" is never so applicable as when one is behind the wheel in Rome. And there is also danger to be had in straying into areas that one shouldn't be in. For instance, in the very centre of Rome there is the Varco Attivo. I once found myself there on my quest to reach the Piazza Navona.'

Melissa laughed comfortably in the front.

The bishop hit the horn again, as a truck forced them towards a car just centimetres away on the left. Sister Veronica shut her eyes.

'Did you have a good sleep, Sister?' Melissa called over her shoulder.

'Not really,' came the terse reply.

'Oh no. I haven't been to sleep at all, just dozed a bit. Definitely a sunglasses day today. Bishop Hammett is taking us to a bed and breakfast he knows.'

'I've stayed there before.' The bishop raised his voice above the hubbub. 'Madame Romano is very helpful and accommodating. But she only has eight rooms; it's a long shot that three will be vacant but I have my fingers crossed that God will smile on us.'

Madam Romano's house was a typical Rome high-rise. Inside it was plain, but clean and welcoming. Sister Veronica was relieved to find three rental rooms were indeed available. She knew she needed to catch up on some sleep soon, she was starting to feel extremely irritable due to her recent lack of it. Bishop Hammett took a room on the third floor, while Melissa and Sister Veronica were given ones on the second floor, where Mme Romano also slept. Half an hour later, all three sat outside the piazza near the bed and breakfast, nursing mugs of steaming black coffee, Melissa's sunglasses firmly in place.

Bishop Hammett stretched, then leaned forward.

'I have a contact in the Vatican that I'm sure that I can trust,' he said. 'He's not high enough to know all the workings of the

Curia and the top leadership, but he is a sympathetic ear. You see, he and I have one very important thing in common. We are both fathers.' He blinked as he said the last four words.

'You acknowledge your child, at least in private.' Sister Veronica could hear the bitterness in her own voice. 'You are a part of her life, you love her and are trying to be a father and a priest. I can see how this torments you, but you should be proud that you are trying.'

'I could not love my daughter more, the thought of disowning her, of not seeing her would be too painful for me to bear. I don't understand those who can do this.' His eyes moistened. 'I often grapple with this conflicting situation I find myself in. I have a child who I love and who I would never change, yet I feel so guilty for this. I promised celibacy and I failed that promise, yet my daughter has brought me more joy than anything. Why is it so hard?'

'It shouldn't have to be,' Melissa said, her eyes narrowing. 'Personally, I think the whole thing's bullshit. Sorry, Sister, but I do. A man has a child. Big deal. Why make him and the child feel so guilty? Other ministers have families, in the Protestant and other faiths, and it doesn't make them any less effective at their jobs. In fact, it probably makes them more effective as they will be able to understand family life more. Catholicism is starting to seem like a big cult to me; separate from your families, disown your children, follow our dogma or be shunned.'

They finished their coffee in silence.

Bishop Hammett shook himself, stretched and stood up.

'Sister, are you up to walking to the Vatican, it's not too far?'

'Yes, yes, the fresh air might wake me up a bit.' She struggled to her feet, smoothing down her skirt.

They set off through streets crowded with tourists and other men and women of the cloth.

'Vatican City is never quiet,' Bishop Hammett said as they walked. 'Everyone who visits Rome wants to see the Vatican at least once. Luckily, as we are "family" we will not have to follow the normal tourist route.'

They walked through ancient courtyards, across a large square, approaching a door where they were admitted after Bishop Hammett showed them his ID. They passed offices, and large rooms with their doors open through which they could see ornate meeting tables. Eventually, they reached a modest-looking office, where Bishop Hammett knocked on the door. There was a shuffling behind the door before it was swung open by a priest, who ushered them inside. Bishop Hammett made the introductions.

'We cannot speak here,' the middle-aged, balding priest, introduced as Father Bianchi, said. 'Let's go to the gardens. If we walk and talk it will appear to onlookers that I am showing you around.'

Filing out of the small office, they followed Father Bianchi to the gardens that turned out to be beautifully tended; full of fountains, sacred sites, and views that made Sister Veronica stop and stare. Passing through several small curated gardens including one comprising solely of cacti, Father Bianchi pointed out a small collection of olive trees. What a truly marvellous harmony between professional gardening and nature's wonders, Sister Veronica mused. This was something exciting, being here in Rome. Much as recent events had tainted and changed her belief in the Catholic Church, being somewhere so magisterial was breathtaking. From almost every spot they could see St Peter's dome, an omnipresent reminder of whose gardens they were in. She couldn't help noting that the beautiful architecture of the dome signposted the power and all-consuming control that had not only shaped the gardens, but the lives of those who lived in the dome's shadow.

As they reached a small fountain with ornately decorated walls flanked by a sculpted figure, Father Bianchi stopped and motioned towards two benches either side of a small pond. Tiny turtles appeared as the group seated themselves.

'I have been working with the office in Paris and have now identified the father of the young man, Jamie, who so cruelly had his life taken from him.'

Sister Veronica nodded appreciatively. She loved it when people got straight to the point.

'Can you tell us who it is?' Bishop Hammett said, leaning forward.

'I can,' the priest said. 'I wish it wasn't true, I believe this man is probably well known to you already. His name is–'

'Father Bianchi!' Loud staccato tones cut across the priest. Sister Veronica looked round – annoyed – at the approaching plump figure in red.

'Father Bianchi. Something has happened and Archbishop Canci wishes to see you in his office this instant.'

'But–'

'This *instant*. Go now. Do not worry, I will continue the tour with these good people.' The man in red was obviously used to being obeyed; he stood there oozing absolute certainty that his bidding would be done.

Shooting Bishop Hammett a desperate look, Father Bianchi stood up and walked off. And there we have it, Sister Veronica thought. Roman Catholic power and control, all siphoned through hierarchy, in action.

They had no choice but to walk with the man, who introduced himself as Bishop Alfonsi, as he headed back towards the dome. Sister Veronica had the distinct impression that they were being herded. Dash it all, they'd been caught so soon. She heard Melissa curse under her breath.

Bishop Alfonsi nodded towards a gate.

'We'll go this way. I take it Father Bianchi has not yet shown you the front of St Peter's Basilica?'

'No, he didn't have a chance,' Sister Veronica said loudly.

She followed the others through the gate, lingering exhaustion slowing her down, and suddenly they were surrounded by people again. A man was walking towards her, carrying two disposable cups balanced on top of each other. He turned to look behind him as he passed. Try as she might to sidestep out of the way, the man marched straight into her, and as he did so dark brown liquid shot out of the cups, drenching her shirt and skirt. The smell of coffee beans saturated her senses.

'Oddio, mi dispiace.' The man raised his hands to his face. 'Prego, scusi. Please, excuse me, I so sorry.'

'Watch what you're doing.' Bishop Alfonsi's voice was back to staccato. 'You are soaked, Sister. This will never do. Please, come with me and I will find someone to help.'

The man, now holding empty containers, backed away, still apologising. But what was that glint of amusement in his eye? Sister Veronica wondered.

Bishop Alfonsi took Sister Veronica's arm and guided her towards a smaller building to the left of St Peter's.

'Please, go inside and have a look round, Sister. We won't be long,' he called over his shoulder to Melissa and Bishop Hammett.

Sister Veronica tried to shake her arm free but Bishop Alfonsi's grip was vice-like, and growing stronger.

'Come with me,' she mouthed to Melissa and Bishop Hammett, but as she turned she saw a man step out of the crowd and block her friends' way; try as they might, they could not pass him. She heard Melissa yell loudly.

Bishop Alfonsi half guided, half dragged her through the small building's entrance, that had a large *No Entry* sign above it, all the time wearing a look of important superiority on his fat face. Guiding her firmly in front of him, he followed her into the dark space, shutting the door behind himself, then bolting it. He pushed her on through the room, his hands gripping her arms like chubby pincers, through a series of doors and corridors, through rooms progressively less magnificent and more shadowy than the previous. They finally came to a halt in a room with no windows. The only light came from a stained-glass panel above the door.

Sister Veronica felt a cold rush of rage.

'What exactly do you think you're doing?'

'Just keeping you safe, Sister. Safe from meddling any further in things you don't understand.' His voice was playful, dangerous.

'I really wouldn't do that if I were you.' Sister Veronica spoke quietly.

'Oh really? And why's that?' Bishop Alfonsi laughed.

Sister Veronica turned and considered the man's arrogant face. There was no warmth in his eyes at all. It was like his soul had been removed. What would appeal to him? What drives him to believe he is so special?

'Because God would not want one of his princes to act in such a way.' It was a long shot but she was willing to try anything.

Bishop Alfonsi's eyes narrowed.

'You, a mere woman, dare to tell me what God wants?' His voice was smooth, steady. 'And how would you know, Sister? Do you have a special hotline to the Lord? Are you closer to him than his apostles?'

Sister Veronica hesitated. Right, so he was a misogynist as well as a deluded bully. The Roman Catholic Church had done its best to exclude women wherever possible, she thought, yet still found they needed them. The resulting conflict between male and female roles, manifested most obviously in the portrayal of men and women in the Bible, left many priests rather confused by women, she'd found. Some were distant, some scared, some friendly, some overly friendly, some normal and some misogynistic. As she stared into his ratty eyes she suspected that females were not the only group Bishop Alfonsi was prejudiced against. He must have detected scepticism on her face as he smiled.

'Ah, I see you do believe this. You are there to serve, Sister. That is all. Service is an important role, you should have stuck to it. It is what you were designed for. But you felt you were more important than this, didn't you? You were not humble. You felt you knew better than Cardinal Moore, you chose to involve yourself in matters meant for men to deal with. You are nothing but a deluded fantasist, Sister. Your actions have disgraced you and harmed many, including God the Almighty. I am here to remind you of your place. It is for your own good. Did you really think you would get away with bringing shame on our beloved church?'

'Our beloved church?' Sister Veronica repeated, thoughts whirring fast through her head. What would be the best angle to take with this man?

'You're right, Your Eminence,' she said, casting her eyes downwards. 'I realised my mistake days ago, and I have been praying hard for forgiveness ever since. I will be obedient from now on, I promise.'

'Do you think I'm a fool, Sister?'

'No, Your Eminence. Not at all.' Yes, a blooming great fat oaf of a fool, she thought. Just look in the mirror and you'll see what I see.

'Yet you expect me to believe you have had a sudden change of heart, a sudden epiphany? Do you think I'm as foolish as you, woman?' A shadow of a smirk crossed Bishop Alfonsi's face.

'Now, I have more important things to attend to, but my two friends here will take good care of you.' He motioned to the darkness behind Sister Veronica. She heard chairs scraping, and footsteps. Two men emerged from the shadows; one look at them told her they were definitely not priests. Their eyes were cold and watchful. One walked towards her, fists full of cable ties, as the bishop slid open the bolts and left, closing the door behind him. The other bolted the door, and pulled a ragged piece of material out of his pocket.

Icy dread coursed down Sister Veronica's spine as the men pushed her backwards onto a chair. She brought her arms up, resisting their rough movements as much as she could but they pressed them back down again, binding them to the sides of the chair with the cable ties, then did the same with her legs. When she opened her mouth to scream, to cry out for the help she so desperately needed, one man shoved the dirty rag into her mouth, and the other roughly applied tape over the top. They stopped to survey their work, then, apparently satisfied, they retreated back into the darkness. Sister Veronica could hear one of them muttering in Italian. The other laughed in reply, an eerie, cruel sound that sent a chill of fear through her.

Try as she might, she could not move. Pain seared through her arms and legs at the points where the ties cut into her flesh.

Breathe slowly, Veronica. She tried to sooth herself. *Keep the airways clear.* But it was too much, and as panic overtook her, silent tears streamed from her eyes. *Well, God*, she thought. *I'm in your hands now.*

32

Cardinal Moore looked up, irritated. Someone was knocking quietly on the door. Ensconced in the sumptuous beauty of a Vatican office, he was taking his thoughts away from the vexing nun by finalising his academic paper, that he had given the working title: *The Historical Contextualisation and Poetic Christian Morality of the Catholic Reasoning of Apostolic Celibacy in Systemic Theology*. It was a shorter, less verbose title than many of his other papers.

'Come in,' he said, partially closing his laptop lid. Bishop Alfonsi entered, drawing up an antique chair on the opposite side of the large desk and squeezing his ample behind into it. The pointed look he gave the near-empty bottle of port was offensive given the amount of wine he himself had drunk last night.

'Did you manage to secure the – er – artefact we were looking for?' Cardinal Moore's tones were smooth, belying his pulse rate. He dared not utter the woman's name too many times within these walls.

Bishop Alfonsi gave a slight nod, a hint of a smile playing on his lips.

'Yes, the – as you call it – artefact is being stored in a location that is very discreet, with no likelihood of being discovered.' He gave a self-satisfied nod.

'Very good.' Cardinal Moore's shoulders relaxed as he breathed out. 'Well done. And what of the charitable donation to the UK? Has that been delivered yet?'

'The donation was received ten minutes ago.' The bishop gave another ghostly smile. 'Everything is fine.'

'What was the delay?'

'It was a minor problem, now neutralised.' Bishop Alfonsi gave the news easily, as though announcing that a relative who had phoned to say they would be late was now happily arriving on time.

'Excellent,' Cardinal Moore said, nodding. *Concordia discors* had been righted, and order would now spring from the moment of confusion, he was sure of it. Events in his world usually ran like clockwork, no matter how big or small, important or trivial they were. And there was no need for deviation from this pleasing path now. His own branches of power reached far enough – with known consequences for people who crossed his will – to ensure that those around him went out of their way to do his bidding with the least amount of fuss. At least this was the case in London. And he was rather looking forward to implementing a similar system in Rome.

33

'Non capisco,' the policeman kept repeating. 'Non capisco, I don't understand.' He glanced at the man, the one who had stepped purposefully out of the crowd and was now suctioned to Melissa and Bishop Hammett's side, who rewarded him with a satisfied nod.

'No, you don't understand. Listen to what I am saying.' Melissa's pulse raced out of control. She ran a hand through her wild hair. 'Someone has taken our friend. A man in red. They went through that door over there and didn't come out. Please help us. Just go and investigate, please.'

'They are all in it together,' Bishop Hammett muttered under his breath. 'Watch their eye contact.'

'Well, we are truly fucked then, aren't we?' Melissa's voice rose as she turned away, shaking, fear taking her over. 'If the police are in on it, who are we supposed to ask for help? Sister Veronica is in danger, they tried to kill her yesterday. What if they've already–' She stopped, unable to finish the sentence, the words too awful to even say. She looked down at the ground, head spinning, running on empty, out of ideas. 'Sod these bloody nicotine patches, I need a real cigarette.' She rubbed her arm ferociously, wishing she'd had the foresight to buy a pack.

Bishop Hammett forced himself to take a deep, slow breath.

'Don't give them the satisfaction of seeing you distressed,' he said in a low voice. 'Let's move away from these people and think about what to do next.'

He took her hand and led her away. Melissa could feel the eyes of the two men searing into her back. Despite her fear, she couldn't help noticing how soft the skin on his hand was, and was reassured by his strong grip. She looked over her shoulder, then frowned.

'They're still watching us,' she muttered.

'Ignore them. It's run Mafia-style here, always has been. But we still have the free will to think and talk. Let's stand here, where they can't see us.' He looked at her white face. 'Do you want to sit down for a minute? I think you might be in shock.'

Melissa nodded. Still holding his hand, she slid down a wall into a crouching position, willing her thoughts to stop reeling; they were making her dizzy. Where the bloody hell had they taken Sister Veronica to? Would she be safe? Why wasn't there anyone in authority they could ask? Guilt and helplessness swam through her, she felt personally responsible for the old nun's safety. She wasn't sure how she'd come to feel so attached to Sister Veronica in the short amount of time they'd known each other, but she felt like an old friend now. Actually, more than that, more like a much-loved relative. And she couldn't bear the thought of anyone mistreating the old lady. The very idea made her feel like throwing up.

'What are we going to do?' she whispered, clenching her fingers until her knuckles turned white. 'God knows what they're doing to her. The police are corrupt. We're being watched. There's nowhere left to turn. Oh God, poor Sister Veronica.' Unspeakable images of what could be happening to the nun flashed through her mind; they were unbearable, painful. Tears leaked from her eyes. 'I'm scared we might never see her again.'

Bishop Hammett took out his phone and tapped the keypad quickly.

'I'm going to call Father Bianchi,' he said. 'Let's see if he can tell us anything.'

34

Sister Veronica woke up with her cheek rammed against her shoulder. Pulling her head upright was downright torture, the muscles had contorted and Saints knew how long she'd been out for. Fear was exhausting, she could remember her eyes closing, she could remember welcoming the darkness as it washed over her, eliminating the terror.

As she stirred, rushes of pins and needles shot down her arms and legs so she stayed still for a moment, orientating herself, willing her blood to pump effectively to those areas that needed it. Thank goodness she'd fallen asleep. Her brain was sharper now, more alert, less addled.

Her eyes grew accustomed to the near darkness. Sister Veronica craned to hear noises, breathing, anything that would identify the presence of her captors; but she heard nothing. Had they gone? It was hard to tell.

Minutes – or perhaps hours – passed; time was a fluid void. Her face felt tight and pinched where the strong tape pulled at the flesh. There was no point moving her arms and legs, the resulting pain was too much to bear. *Have faith, Veronica*, she told herself. *There are more forces at work in this world than we can comprehend, don't assume the worst will happen. And if it does, it's not the end. You know it's not. Death is a door to pass through, not a finality.*

Primal fear kept rearing its snake-like head, and for unidentifiable amounts of time her head whirled with terror. But terror would not win, she was sure of that. So she played her favourite hymns and Christmas carols round in her brain until each time the panic subsided.

Her stomach growled and ached. And she desperately needed to empty her bladder. Drat, damn and double-blasted hell.

The ongoing silence in the room must mean the men were either asleep or absent. She tried making some muffled noises out loud, and still there was no hint of additional human presence.

Then a sound, a metallic fumbling from the dark recesses of the room, like someone was trying to open an internal door. Instantly, adrenaline flooded back through her veins and her skin bristled.

Hurried footsteps approaching, then:

'Oh, Sister Veronica, what have they done to you?'

It was Father Bianchi's voice. Feeling a surge of gladness as his distraught face came into view in the gloom, Sister Veronica sent a heartfelt prayer of thanks to the cosmos. Father Bianchi – his thin fingers trembling – peeled away the tape from her mouth, and removed the rag, shaking his head, tears at the corners of his eyes.

'We don't have much time,' he whispered, bending down to untie her arms and legs. 'Are you okay, Sister? What did they do to you?'

'Oh, I'll live.' Sister Veronica flexed her aching arms. 'Bishop Alfonsi was here. He kindly left two thugs to take care of me, they were the ones who tied me up.'

'The bishop is a wicked man,' Father Bianchi muttered, pulling the cable ties away and throwing them to the side. 'The thugs are groundsmen here, they have gone outside to smoke cigarettes. They are clearly in his pay. So much corruption exists here, in this *holy* place. Bishop Hammett called me but I couldn't answer, as too many people were near me. So instead I received a text from him about what happened to you. I know these rooms very well, when he told me the door you were taken through I thought they would bring you here, to the depths of the labyrinth, it's so soundproof and unused. I've been watching and waiting for an hour. There, all done. Can you stand up, Sister? Here, give me your hands and I will help you.'

'Yes, it's fine, I can walk,' Sister Veronica said, as she stood up slowly. Apart from the searing pain in her calves where the cable ties had left their mark, her legs worked well.

'Quick, we must hurry. Here, take these papers, Sister. If anything happens to me again, it's important you have them. They contain the information you are looking for.' Father Bianchi withdrew a fold of documents from his pockets, and thrust them at Sister Veronica, who fumbled for them in the near darkness. Once her fingers had closed round them she swiftly deposited them in the deep pockets of her skirt.

'Thank you,' she said, following him as he turned towards the blackness at the back of the room. 'Really. You've saved my life.'

'I'm glad,' Father Bianchi whispered. 'It seems I have done something useful for once. Now follow me. We must not talk now. We must go this way and hope we make it. Too many watchers are at the front of the building.'

Stopping and starting, going further into the dark recesses of the room, they finally reached the door, and Father Bianchi pushed it open.

A man stood there. For a split second Sister Veronica

wondered if she was imagining things, but she recognised his scarred face immediately – one of her captors.

'Ciao,' he said, holding up a knife.

'Run, Sister,' Father Bianchi shouted, grabbing the man's arm, twisting the knife away. 'Go, go now!'

Sister Veronica hesitated, panic searing through her.

'GO!' roared Father Bianchi, squirming as the thug bent the knife back towards his throat.

She went as she was bid, running into the darkness, sending up a prayer of protection for her rescuer, then flinching as she heard Father Bianchi cry out, an animalistic noise that echoed through the corridor. She stopped, the feeling that maybe she should double back and help the priest tearing at her insides. It just wasn't fair that he should be hurt so she could be saved. But yet, there was something bigger going on in the church that would be successfully silenced if she did not make it out of Rome alive. The fear, the anger, the guilt, the desperate helplessness in her was overwhelming and her nails dug into her palms as she tried to think about what was best to do. No, she must go further, she decided. For Jamie and all the other children of clergy. So on and on she went, the conflict about her choice, the fact that she'd left Father Bianchi behind, burning in her brain.

She felt the walls on either side of her. There was a door here, was it safe to open it? She didn't know, couldn't tell. So she ran on, further into the blackness, until she hit a wall. Her fingers fumbled, trying to read what was in front of her. Another door, a fastened bolt. Her fingers shaking, she slid back the bolt and found a stairwell before her, bathed in murky light. She had no option, she knew, she must go down the stairs to whatever fate awaited her.

The light came from grilles in the walls. A cold, damp smell reminded her of her grandfather's cellar. At the bottom of the stairs was a room full of stacked chairs, rows of folded tables, broken statues and piles of boxes, all grey and eerie in the dim light. A door, again bolted. She grabbed an old piece of material that covered a fractured mirror and threw it over her head, an ad hoc headscarf would have to do, she needed some sort of disguise. Pushing the papers even further down in her pocket, she drew the bolts back and stepped outside, her head bowed, the mildewed material swinging round her shoulders.

Finding herself in a distinctly less magnificent courtyard than those on display in the Vatican Gardens, Sister Veronica walked past piles of cigarette butts, listening to washing machines and tumble dryers whir behind nearby walls. Some windows were open, and she walked past these as quickly as she could. As she went on, the murmur and hubbub of the crowds of sightseers got louder and through a gap between two buildings she spied a group of Japanese tourists, cameras at the ready, chattering happily.

Inching forward, headscarf pulled closely around her face, Sister Veronica surveyed the scene in front of St Peter's Basilica. A few seconds later she spotted a man she thought was the henchman that had deterred Melissa and Bishop Hammett from following her. He had his back to her, and was clearly staring at something, but she recognised his black jacket, greasy hair and bouncer-like stance. Daring herself to poke her head round the corner, she saw his visual targets; Melissa, white and drawn, next to Bishop Hammett, who was talking frantically into his phone.

Compulsively patting the papers in her pocket again, Sister Veronica felt a hard lump at the bottom. A pen. She always carried one, never knew when she would need it, usually for writing ideas for her crime books on scraps of paper and napkins. And thank goodness for that. Drawing it out, she carefully took out the folded papers, and tore off a strip of blank white at the bottom of the last page. Much as she yearned to read their contents now, the documents would have to wait until later.

MEET ME AT THE CAR, she wrote, before folding the paper up and depositing the rest of the stash deeply back in her pocket.

Retracing her steps to the storage room she had exited the building from, she fished around and collected a bundle of drapes and rags that covered other old items, quickly folding them into a rough pile, her nose wrinkling at their damp smell. Rearranging her headscarf into the most convincing style she could manage, with a good deal covering her face, Sister Veronica picked up her pile of materials, her folded note clutched tightly in one fist. You're a washerwoman, she told herself. You work here. Don't keep looking around, don't look guilty. Just stare straight ahead.

Stooping slightly, and adopting a limping gait, she came once again to the gap between the buildings.

Right, Veronica. Into the lions' den.

35

The British Vatican contact exited the Wessex Building Society and immediately became anonymous in suburban London's insalubrious Hounslow High Street. Strolling past a gang of teenagers drinking cheap beer from cans, he reflected how easy it was to carry out these jobs he was tasked with by his Vatican comrades. No questions were ever asked of a priest in banks, people just trusted you wherever you went. It was all so smooth and effortless. His phone rang.

'Yes?'

'Is it all safe?' Cardinal Moore asked.

'Oh very safe indeed. The tea has not only been made but poured successfully and handed out,' the man in Hounslow said.

'Excellent.'

'Has the other problem been cleared up?' The British contact cleared his throat. It puzzled him as to why this particular clean-up had taken so long. She was just a woman, how hard could it be to stop her? If he'd been there...

'I believe so.'

'Very good.'

'God bless.'

'God bless, Father.'

The British contact put his phone in his pocket, and smiled as he walked.

36

Melissa stared straight ahead, eyes wide, listening to Chris talking to Dominique. People going about their tourist activities looked so happy and content around her. How could they be living such different lives to her? Be feeling such opposite emotions? They were so lucky to be enjoying their time in Vatican City in such carefree ways.

'Yes, we know it was Simone,' he was saying, turning away and staring out at the gardens. 'Bloody traitor. No, we don't know where Sister Veronica has been taken. We have our own spies watching us, we can't get near the buildings, we've tried. Yes, I've phoned and texted Father Bianchi but he hasn't replied yet. They are watching him too, he was called away with some poor excuse that he was needed somewhere.'

An old woman hobbled towards them, carrying a pile of washing. Melissa observed her limp past their watchful guard, heading for a nearby gate. As she came closer, the old woman slowly lifted her head.

Sister Veronica! Thank bloody God, she's still alive.

Careful not to change her facial expression in any way,

Melissa turned towards the dome, squinting. A smell of musty material wafted past as Sister Veronica shuffled on, and Melissa felt the gentlest tap on her shoe. Glancing down, she saw a fold of paper had landed there. She waited a few minutes, still pretending to scrutinise the dome of St Peter's, before getting her notebook out of her pocket, pretending to fumble with it, then dropping it next to her feet. Bending down, she retrieved not only the notebook, but the folded paper. She opened it.

MEET ME AT THE CAR, she read.

Good work, Sister, ten out of ten for acting ability, you old superstar.

Heart pounding, Melissa withdrew her phone from her pocket, thanking her lucky stars that she had decided to ask Chris for his number the day before.

Don't ask me any questions now but we need to get back to the car, she texted him. *Sister Veronica's going to meet us there. I'll explain everything on the way.*

'Okay, okay, I'll let you know if anything changes, Dominique,' he was saying. 'Yes I agree, this is all a nightmare. Please do let me know if you hear anything. Right, stay in touch, bye for now.'

'Received any new texts?' Melissa murmured.

Chris looked down at his phone, then put it in his pocket.

'There doesn't seem to be any point in us staying around here,' he said, stretching. 'What do you think?'

The man watching looked interested, and took a step forward.

'No, I think you're right.' Melissa sighed and rubbed her eyes. 'I'm so tired. Shall we go back to the bed and breakfast for a bit?'

'Good idea.' Chris took her trembling hand, and led her out through the gate.

He's following us, Melissa thought, as Sister Veronica's back view disappeared into a side street. The footsteps behind them got louder and closer.

37

Cardinal Moore, basking in the praise of the special committee – SB9, set up to investigate the ordained involved in the clerical abuse scandal – found Bishop Alfonsi's entrance rather unwelcome. Those who sat on the council were handpicked by the Pope to give him advice and guidance on critical matters that related to the future of the Catholic Church. The Pope had given instructions to SB9 that he wanted help in identifying any cardinals that the council may do better without. Two cardinals, including the one investigated by Cardinal Moore had been written to and thanked for their service and a third cardinal had also been dismissed by His Holiness and although age may have been the explanation given, it was widely known that the decision to dismiss had been due to far more than just advancing years. The highest-ranking prelate whose name had been linked with a sex scandal abroad had been granted an indefinite leave of absence, and Cardinal Moore had his eyes firmly set on the opportunity that his superior's time off presented. He was very pleased with the outcome of his investigation. He had handled it in the delicate manner that was required, and had done an excellent job. He felt that at last he was being appreciated for the skills he possessed. He had even had a handwritten note from the Pope himself, expressing his gratitude. He was important, a prince.

'My apologies, but Cardinal Moore is urgently needed.' Bishop Alfonsi's voice was smooth but his eyes dripped with darkness.

'Of course.' The elderly Cardinal in charge smiled benignly and waved his hand, before turning back to his business.

Cardinal Moore sighed, then stood up.

'She's gone,' Bishop Alfonsi spat when they were alone in the corridor, his stomach wobbling with the force of his words.

'What? But that's impossible.' Cardinal Moore's voice was loud.

'Father Bianchi went in to release her when Gioele and Filippo went out for a cigarette. He told me he needed to go to the bathroom but he never came back, he must have worked out where she was being held and went straight there. Gioele returned in time to find them leaving, but Father Bianchi apprehended him, and ended up getting stabbed. He's now fighting for his life in hospital, I don't expect him to last the night. We immediately minimised the scandal, of course, explained to the police that Gioele went mad and stabbed him and that he must be suffering from a mental illness. He's now in custody.'

'That woman is dangerous,' Cardinal Moore growled, remembering to keep his tones low. 'She knows too much about the death of Jamie Markham. She needs to be stopped. As you know, it's not just about Jamie, it's about protecting our financial source in Britain. There's too much at stake here.'

'Yes, I know, we understand that,' Bishop Alfonsi muttered. 'But she's proving difficult to hold.'

'Next time, don't hold her. Finish the business once and for all immediately. Understood?' Cardinal Moore had never given such an order before, but he was surprised how good it made him feel.

'Yes, Your Eminence. It will be done. And this time she will be made to suffer greatly for the inconvenience she has caused.'

38

'You have everything in your power again, Veronica,' the nun told herself, puffing along, not daring to look around or remove her damp-smelling headscarf. 'You are free, you are safe. Now find the blessed car, for goodness' sake.' Not used to this much exercise all in one go, her breaths were coming out as wheezes, and her lungs hurt. It had been a hard day, pain-wise, she reflected. The places where the cable ties had dug in would be sore for weeks. The guilt about leaving Father Bianchi behind still burned in her head and heart. She felt sure he could never have survived the attack and if he'd died to save her she would be eternally humbled and mortified at such a heroic deed, and appalled because it was for her and she wasn't worthy enough for any person to give their life for her.

The street she turned down was quiet, soothing. Everything about it felt ordered; the windows and doors along the smooth buildings were evenly spaced apart, as were the trees, even the parking spaces. It was neat, precise and mathematical. Very unlike my brain at this exact moment, Sister Veronica thought, wishing the pounding ache in her head would go away. It was taking all her self-control not to stop and read the papers that

Father Bianchi had passed to her, that still lay deep in her pockets, she checked on them multiple times. How desperately she needed to know the information they contained. But now was not the time, they all needed to get to safety first, and at the moment that seemed an intangibly long way away.

All the streets she turned down were similar; calm and grand, the grasp of the all-powerful Vatican – owners of the entire city – evident at all times. The architecture – that had seemed beautiful earlier – started to take on an air of ostentatious fakery, and her desire to leave Rome intensified.

'Where's the dratted car?' she muttered under her breath as she turned down yet another road, madly eyeballing all the vehicles. 'I must be going round in circles. They all look the dashed same.' Cursing her inability to recognise anything, she stomped on, feeling hotter and more annoyed with each step. Her head turned as she scanned the streets, looking over her shoulder every few seconds, aware of the grave danger she was in, wondering how her life had become so complicated and terrifying.

She rounded the corner and a familiar sight greeted her eyes; the Fiat Cinquecento she'd slept so uncomfortably in. As she gazed through the window at their packed bags huddled together on the back seat, she rejoiced at Bishop Hammett's earlier request that they take all their belongings from the bed and breakfast in case a quick getaway was needed. Sensible man, Sister Veronica thought. She could quite understand why Melissa couldn't take her eyes off him.

For the first time since throwing the note at Melissa, a pang of uncertainty shivered through her. It had been a long shot, but the only thing she could think of at the time. What if they hadn't read the note for some reason? What if they couldn't get away from their guard? He did seem rather attached to them, like Velcro. What if the powers that be captured them in her place, angry that she'd escaped? *No*, she told herself sternly. *Stop it this instant, Veronica. Never ever lose hope, do you hear me?* Even so, she couldn't stop her eyes from frantically flitting up and down the street. Where were they, for dashed sake? Surely they wouldn't be that far behind her if they'd read the note? They must have read the note! Please God, let them have read the blessed note.

Suddenly, the sound of running footsteps resounded through the streets. It was such an ill-fitting, vulgar noise in the staid, respectable environment that she looked up instantly. Melissa and the bishop came tearing round the corner, Bishop Hammett immediately pressing the key fob's button and unlocking the car.

One look at the sweat running down their strained faces told Sister Veronica all she needed to know, and she threw herself onto the back seat, pushing the bags to the floor, slamming the door behind her. Melissa jumped onto the passenger seat at the same time as Bishop Hammett arrived behind the wheel. He immediately started the engine, revved the gas, and the car screeched away.

'You were being followed by that oaf, I presume?' Sister Veronica said, after their frantic breathing had slowed.

'Yes,' Melissa said, wiping her forehead, swivelling round. 'That bloody man was trailing us but we nipped down an alley and managed to buy ourselves a few seconds of freedom. Oh, Sister, I'm so glad you're okay. What happened to you? Did they hurt you?' She stared at Sister Veronica, tears leaking from her eyes, scanning her friend for signs of injury or mistreatment.

As Sister Veronica filled them in on her capture and escape, and the bravery of poor Father Bianchi, and assured Melissa that she would live to fight another day, Bishop Hammett drove them out of Vatican City and on to faster roads. Twinges of relief started to dissolve the rigid tension between all of them as they covered more ground, putting much welcomed distance between them and the Vatican.

'But Father Bianchi did manage to give me some documents before we ran into that thug.' On the back seat, Sister Veronica delved into her pocket and retrieved the papers. 'He knew he was taking his life in his hands by coming to find me; he said the papers would provide us with important information *if anything happened to him*. My heart almost broke when I heard him cry out but he'd told me to go, so I honoured his wishes. Was it the right thing to do, I wonder? That lovely man saved my life, and one day I'd like to thank him in person but I'm so afraid he won't have survived, the man attacking him was savage, evil. If Father Bianchi died on my account I will never get over it. But now we must force ourselves to concentrate on this or his actions will have been in vain. Too much is at stake for any of us to fall apart now. We can only hope these papers contain information that will help end this horror and give poor Jamie's family some closure.'

Heart pounding, dread and optimism at what she might find coursing through her in equal measure, she opened the crumpled pile and began to read. The first grainy, photocopied sheet was filled with barely legible curly writing.

To anyone who this matter may concern, I have been advised to write a brief note explaining the arrangements made for the care of baby Jamie Markham. Jamie's natural father, named–

Sister Veronica dropped the papers. A tidal wave of nausea heaved through her. No. It couldn't be. Not this person. Please, not him. With shaking hands, she lifted up the paper and reread the name of Jamie's father. There it was, in black and white. She reread it, then read it again, to be sure. Pain stabbed through her heart, splintering it into fragments, as slabs of understanding fell into place in her head.

Melissa swivelled round and stared.

'Are you okay, Sister?' she asked. 'You look very ill. Maybe you're having a delayed reaction to all the stress. Try and have a sleep while Chris drives.'

'Get us safely to London, Bishop.' Sister Veronica's voice came out strained, almost strangled. 'There's something I have to do. I understand everything now.' She put her head in her hands and wept huge gulping sobs of shock and grief.

39

'Well, where is she?' the British contact said.

'They were tracked to Paris, then Gerardo lost sight of them.' Archbishop Canico's tones were apologetic and soothing, hiding his fury at the incompetence of his team. 'I'm so very sorry.'

There was silence as the British contact considered this. Then an exasperated exhalation of breath. The woman was resourceful. But then he'd always known she was intelligent. It was regrettable that she had to die, but by now she would probably have information that would end his career, and also expose the extent of his private dealings with the Vatican. And he simply could not allow that to happen.

'I have an idea where she'll be heading,' the British contact said. 'I will deal with this matter myself now. It will be closed down in twenty-four hours.' Cardinal Moore had let him down; failed, in fact. He wouldn't hesitate to make it very clear. As suspected, the man wasn't ready for this kind of responsibility. He'd tried to tell them at the Vatican, but they'd insisted on giving him a chance.

'Very good,' came the reply. 'And you were right, by the way, Charles isn't up to the job.'

The British contact smiled. It was very rare for him to ever be wrong about these things.

40

There was a queue for the Eurostar.

Melissa watched Sister Veronica, a feeling of sorrow in her heart. So much had happened to the old woman over the last week, yet she still carried on bravely. But since finding out who Jamie's father was – a fact she'd shared with herself and Chris during the long car journey – the nun had aged ten years. She seemed shrunken, not just in stature but in energy and drive. It was horrible seeing her reduced to this after she'd fought through so much.

'She'll be okay,' Chris whispered in her ear, his fingers mingling with her own, his breath soft on her neck. 'She's grieving for the friend she thought she had. It's a terrible shock to find out you've been deceived for years, almost worse than losing a loved one to death. She'll bounce back, she's a tough cookie. Just give her some time.'

Melissa fought off the claustrophobic feeling she was getting from the tightly-packed queue by letting her thoughts drift to her connection with Chris. Bishop Hammett. Was she actually fucking insane, or was she seriously having feelings for an ordained priest; not just a priest, a bishop? But... he was just a human being, like she was. And he seemed ten million times more loveable than those fake priests who pretended to be something they were not; clones of Jesus himself in public and dark manipulators obsessed with status and power in private. If her experiences over the last few days had taught her anything, it was how important the intent in someone's heart was. Not the show they put on to the outside world, but the actual love or hate they held inside them, that defined everything about who they really were. Because that was what mattered, right? Chris was conflicted, sure. And he hadn't always made the wisest life decisions, but who had? But his motive for leading a double life for quite some time was love; love for his child (and for a time her mother), and love for the church and God. But the other wolves in sheep's clothing, pretending to be good priests and getting the masses to love them, but in reality being cold-blooded killers, or having evil intent, or hypocrites, liars, dishonest unsavoury deceivers who valued money and power above goodness, now that was heinous to the highest degree. It wasn't just hypocritical, it was revolting and abominable, the highest abuse of power she could imagine. Poor Jamie, he hadn't stood a chance.

At last, they boarded the packed train and found their seats, bending themselves into unnatural angles as they attempted to sit down while impatient commuters pushed past.

'Melissa,' Sister Veronica said, leaning forward as Chris loaded their bags up onto the overhead rack. 'I must ask you something. Do you have any contacts in the newspaper industry that would let you work for them? Publish a front-page story of great interest? I have been thinking, and I believe we have to expose Jamie's murder and his father for who he really is in the national press. There is too much subterfuge in the Catholic Church, too much pretence, dishonesty and hypocrisy. And as we have found out, there is a cold-hearted killer who is prepared to end the life of a priest's son purely to protect jobs, reputations and corrupt goings-on.'

Melissa nodded.

'Yes, I know a few editors. What would you like me to say to them?'

'Tell them everything we know so far. Tell them about Jamie's murder, and who his father is. I have a feeling that by the time I have finished my next task in London, we will know with certainty who Jamie's killer is too, and we need to add that to the story.'

Melissa reached for her handbag, retrieving her notebook, pen and mobile phone. Sister Veronica's 'next task' in London sounded rather ominous, but she knew she would be unlikely to get an answer at this stage if she pressed her friend on exactly what it was she had planned. Still, she was glad some colour had come back into Sister Veronica's cheeks, and that she was talking of future plans again.

'Right,' she said, as the train purred into action. 'Leave it with me. I'm going to make some calls, then I need you to give me a detailed account of everything you want in the article, don't leave anything out.'

41

Cardinal Moore groaned as he turned off his phone and threw it on to his desk. Without even noticing what he was doing, he picked up the bottle of port and drained it completely empty. Wiping his mouth with the back of his hand, he considered how Bishop Alfonsi had taken rather too much delight for his liking in telling him Sister Veronica was still free and on the move, and that their contact in Britain – who was in the midst of rolling out their new monetary scheme – had taken charge of dispatching her himself. This was not pleasing news in the slightest, as Cardinal Moore had a fearful respect for the man in question, and had been angling to keep in his good books. Now, as the bloody woman was still on the run, he would look incompetent. And he, Cardinal Moore, was never, ever incompetent – in public at least. How does that woman keep surviving? He banged the desk with his fist.

The only ray of light in the tedious situation was that Henri had phoned just before with the news that the official canon law investigation into Jamie Markham's death by the assessors had now been neatly wrapped up, with a copy of the finished report waiting for him in London. At least one section of his life was still running smoothly.

Packing his bag, with much less zeal than he had done for his outgoing trip to Rome, Cardinal Moore reflected on his meeting with Matteo at breakfast. If he hadn't been mistaken, his good friend had been a little distant with him. Almost cold. Not for the first time over the last twenty-four hours, Cardinal Moore wondered if something was going on that he wasn't party to. There was something in Matteo's manner that made him concerned, and feel a little vulnerable perhaps; a sensation he hadn't felt for decades. But what could it be? They were in this together; princes, the chosen ones. Friends, for goodness' sake. They needed money to continue their mission as shepherds of the people; to ensure they remained all-powerful beings. They weren't doing anything corrupt, they were following in the age-old Vatican tradition of producing wealth from nothing, weren't they? They were doing this to ensure the long survival of their traditional institution and them as men of God in these modern times. Matteo wouldn't do anything unpleasant to him behind his back. Would he? And he would have surely corrected the *Nota relative alla prassi della Congregazione per il Clero a proposito dei chierici con prole*, regarding that particular parental matter of children of the ordained. Wouldn't he? Because if he hadn't, and the old bat, Sister Veronica had somehow got her hands on that highly sensitive information, then he – Cardinal Moore – was in the deadliest of trouble. Not least with the British contact in charge of their monetary scheme. A cold sweat broke out all over his body.

42

'We're here.' Melissa looked out of the window at the London station. 'Blimey, when did it get so dark? It must be past ten o'clock.'

People traipsed past them in dribs and drabs; some clearly out for the night and some going home to bed. Strange how normal life went on when your world was collapsing around you, Sister Veronica reflected. It seemed both insulting and comforting at the same time.

She glanced at Melissa, then shrugged, too tense to speak. Forcing her features into relative composure, she swallowed down the nausea that had threatened to undo her since first reading that name; Jamie's father's name. How could he? How *could* he do this? It was unthinkable, yet it was real.

'The *Daily News* is expecting my copy of the story any time before midnight. Ethan said he'd have it on the front page of tomorrow's paper if we get it to him in time.' Melissa stood up, reaching for the bags, distributing them around.

Sister Veronica nodded.

'Thank you,' she managed. 'Thank you both for everything. But I must go on alone now. There's something I must find out, and I don't want either of you to get into any more trouble.'

'No way,' Melissa said firmly. 'I'm not leaving you by yourself. I'm not being rude, Sister, but you look terrible. There's no way we're letting you go on alone, especially at this time of night.'

'Charming, I'm sure.' A flash of Sister Veronica's old self returned and a smile played on her lips.

'Melissa's right,' Bishop Hammett said kindly. 'You do look exhausted, Sister, and quite understandably so, with the ordeal you've been through. Please. Let us come with you. It's the least we can do, with all the effort you're putting into this.'

Sister Veronica raised her eyes to heaven.

'All right,' she said. 'I know you are both being kind and want to look after me. I don't mean to be ungrateful, but I would feel terrible if anything happened to either of you on my account. However, before we go, I must get a bottle of water from that shop over there. I'm awfully thirsty.' She gestured towards a newsagent's store at the side of the platform. 'Would either of you like anything?'

Receiving polite answers in the negative, she walked away and Melissa watched as her friend disappeared through the shop's entrance.

She slid her arms through Chris's, and they waited, hugging each other.

'Chris, something's not right,' Melissa said after a few minutes, drawing away, craning to see into the shop. 'I can just feel it. I need to go and check on her.'

'I'll come with you,' Bishop Hammett said, frowning, and seconds later they were scouting round the near-empty shop, walking up and down the aisles of chocolates, sweets, crisps, drinks and newspapers. Only three other people turned out to be in the shop; two teenagers dressed in clubbing gear and the man serving behind the counter. But no Sister Veronica. There was another door on the other side of the shop, that led out on to the busy Euston Road.

'Oh my God, where the bloody hell has she gone?' Melissa's voice rose as she stared at the door, her pulse quickening. 'Has she given us the slip on purpose? She wouldn't do that, would she?'

43

Father John let go of his vice-like grip on Sister Veronica's wrist as he pushed her on to the back seat of his car. She tumbled sideways, her cheek hitting an armrest.

'That's right, Veronica, get your feet in, there's a good girl. We wouldn't want you to get hurt now, would we?' His voice was still soft and calm, the same as it had always been, but as Sister Veronica looked up and saw his eyes illuminated by a street light, she recoiled. There was not one bit of kindness left in them; instead, they swam with anger and malice. How had she got the man so wrong? And for all these years? She must still be in shock about the whole affair, or she wouldn't have been so stupid as to be caught as soon as she arrived in London. Yet she still couldn't believe it. Father John. John. Her friend, her companion, the one person she talked to – apart from Agnes – when she felt down or had a problem. But she had been mistaken. She stamped her foot down hard. Duped and hoodwinked by a bad man pretending to be good. How could this have happened? How on earth could she have been so ignorantly stupid? She felt like bashing her head against the car window.

'We're just going for a little drive now, Veronica,' Father John said pleasantly, clicking on the internal locking system as the car slid away. Honky-tonk jazz came on the car radio, and Sister Veronica shut her eyes for a second; the contrast between the merry beats and her dark situation felt too incongruously awful. But then, perhaps John intended to taunt her in this way. Maybe he'd lined up the radio station beforehand; anything seemed possible now. 'My goodness, you have been busy, haven't you? Led quite a few people on a merry dance, so I'm told. Good for you, shows spirit. And it's a great last memory for you to have. Your last hurrah, if you will.' He chuckled.

Sister Veronica's mind whirred.

'A great last memory, John?' she said. 'Has it really come to that?'

John glanced at her in the driver's mirror as they slowed to a halt in busy London traffic. Horns beeped all around. She tried to open the car door but the central locking system held fast.

'You know exactly what needs to happen now, Veronica. And really, it's your own fault. You've had so many chances to leave things alone, to take your nose out of other people's business. But you had to keep going on, didn't you? Tracking down your own version of the truth like a demented bloodhound.' He ground his teeth together, his face suddenly ugly.

'My version of the truth?' The anger within Sister Veronica boiled over as the car lurched forward again. 'MY version of the truth? No, John, you evil man. The truth is the truth. You can't manipulate it to please yourself, despite what you think.' She paused, summoning up the energy to say her next words.

'You killed your own son, didn't you?'

Father John sighed.

'I don't suppose it matters if I tell you now,' he said and for a moment his eyes in the car mirror flickered. What had passed across them? Regret? Shame? 'Yes, sadly Jamie had to go, although it wasn't something I enjoyed, and in truth I hoped it would never come to that. I don't know whether you will believe me about this, Veronica, but it's true. I would never have initiated such a serious course of action had it not been totally necessary. I was there at the hostel that day although I didn't actually perform the act of *interfectio* myself. I couldn't have done that. The fact is that Jamie was a damaged creature for many years. I had people watching him, keeping an eye on him, of course, as he grew up. He was never an outgoing sort of boy, always too shy. And then when that busybody – I never succeeded in finding out who – sent him a note saying he was the son of a priest, well, Jamie really deteriorated then. He became bent on finding out my identity, self-harming all the while, and in the end he succeeded. He was planning on telling you what he knew, the day you found his body. I believe he had idealised notions of trying to get me to step down as a priest, and to be a father to him. Of course, that was absolutely out of the question, and it very sadly led to his demise.'

'And how do you know all this?' Sister Veronica's voice was thick with emotion. The despair at what her former friend had become was overwhelming.

'The silly boy sent me a pitiful note, asking why I hadn't been a father to him for all these years. Asking what was wrong with him, why I couldn't love him, why I hadn't got to know him when he was little.' Father John sighed. 'Of course I couldn't have done that, could I?'

Sister Veronica sat silently, refusing to meet the priest's gaze in the mirror.

They set off again, moving haltingly through London's busy streets. Around them young people laughed on the pavements and businessmen and women spilled out of pubs.

'And Sister Anastasia?' she said eventually. 'Presumably, you finished her off in the hospital because she heard you killing Jamie?'

'Indeed she did,' Father John agreed. 'She was blind, but not stupid. She must have heard my companion and I talking. I suspected she may have which is why I went to visit her at the hospital; the fact that she was there made it easier really. The poor dear was so near death, I actually did her a kindness. It didn't take long, she was gone in seconds. She would have died anyway, she was very ill. You could say that I just speeded up the process.'

'She told me she knew who murdered Jamie when I was alone with her for a few moments in the hospital.' Sister Veronica dug her nails into the palms of her hands. 'But not who did it. I can't believe I didn't work it out.' She sent up a quick prayer and apology to Sister Anastasia, in case she was listening.

'You're a smart woman, Veronica,' Father John said. 'You've done better than most would have on this adventure of yours. I heard you even got the better of Bishop Alfonsi; he'll be fuming about that for weeks.' He sighed. 'Look, we've had some great times together, and believe me, I won't take any pleasure in what has to happen when we get there. Like I said before, I never wanted things to turn out like this. But because of you and Jamie I've been left with no choice.'

'When we get where?'

'You'll see.'

44

'Did you see an old woman in here just a few minutes ago?' Bishop Hammett spoke urgently to the bored-looking man behind the counter. 'She was carrying a satchel? Wearing a skirt and blouse? Fairly short with a wide build? Please, this is important, we really need to find her.'

'Yeah.' The young man looked up from his phone, leaving a game to play itself out. 'An old man came in and said their taxi was waiting, then he took her wrist and dragged her out. I thought it was a bit off, but you see all sorts of things here. I never get involved.'

'Chris, we've got to find her, she's in terrible danger.' Melissa's voice cracked as she punched three nines into her phone's keypad. 'She would have told us if she was meeting someone, I know she would have. I'm phoning the police right now.'

'Yes, you do that while I ring round the people I know who could help us.' Bishop Hammett's hands shook as he reached into his jacket pocket.

'Hello?' Melissa said, as the man behind the counter stared

at her with interest. 'Yes, I need the police. A friend of mine has been kidnapped, we think it was by a priest called Father John. Please, you have to help us.'

45

Cardinal Moore stared straight ahead as the plane took off, pondering the strange conversation he'd had with Bishop Alfonsi just before his departure from the Vatican. Unusually, the bishop had come to bid him farewell.

'You can cancel your flight here next month, Cardinal. You won't be needed at the next meeting after all.' A slight smirk had played around the man's lips at this point.

'But I have the tickets all booked!' Cardinal Moore remembered saying. 'And surely the monies will have been deposited in our accounts by then? Aren't we all going to go out to celebrate? I was told by Matteo that the restaurant has been booked.' He had been looking forward to that; a public celebration with powerful men – his friends – from the Vatican.

'Ah,' Bishop Alfonsi had replied. 'Well, you may find yourself a little more busy than usual in the coming weeks. Don't feel the need to come here if you are, er, all tied up.' There had been no one else there to observe this odd little incident, which the Cardinal found disconcerting in itself. There was an air of untethering going on, a feeling of being detached and pushed away, but without any tangible reasons or explanations. He refused to entertain the notion that he was becoming paranoid; he'd always abhorred those with so-called mental illnesses whining about their pain. But up until now his life had blossomed in the way he deserved and he could not fathom the thought that something would put a stop to this. Then the taxi had arrived before he could think any more about it.

Matteo hadn't come to say goodbye, and that had stung more than it should. Something was definitely going on, something wasn't right, and it made Cardinal Moore feel a strange emotion. What was it now? Fear. Yes, that was it.

He motioned to the air steward, who came forward politely.

'Yes, sir, can I help you?'

'A large double brandy,' Cardinal Moore said, his face sagging.

46

F ather John smiled kindly as he watched Sister Veronica struggle. Another man had come out of the shadows behind her and was now grasping her wrist tightly with one hand, while pressing the cold barrel of a shotgun into her neck with the other. Her chest heaved up and down rapidly, her breathing constricted by anger and fear.

They were standing in the warm night air amidst derelict warehouses. The only lights were the car headlights Father John had left turned on. The drive had been painfully slow for the most part, and Sister Veronica was distinctly annoyed with how terrified she'd felt. Right now, the emotion of anger was battling ferociously with that of dread, each trying to become the front runner.

'John,' she said, knowing this was her last chance to change his mind. 'Please stop and consider what you're about to do, just for a minute. Don't pursue this course of action, John, I'm asking you from the very essence of my heart. Think about yourself. If you do this, it will inevitably lead to your own destruction. Can't you see that?'

Father John, standing in front of her, shrugged his shoulders.

'I'm sorry,' he said. 'It has to happen like this Veronica. There is no other way forward at this point.'

Then anger surged up inside her, as she stared into her former friend's eyes, and something that had been growing inside her since her capture exploded.

'I may die tonight, but you won't have won,' she hissed at Father John. 'You're a coward, John. And the worst sort of evil human being. I wholly believe death is not the end of our journey, and once your time comes you will have greater forces to answer to than your obedient little subjects on this earth.' She lurched forward but the man holding her forced her back so hard she yelped.

'Oh, Veronica, how delightful. Still so zealous to the end.' Father John rubbed his hands together. 'Right, we won't drag the moment on longer than we need to. God bless you, my dear, may you sleep well. Darius, when you're ready?' He motioned to his companion.

The full realisation of her situation occurring, Sister Veronica steadied herself, knowing there was nothing more she could do. She quietly offered thanks for her life to the universe and anyone else who was listening, glad for the sense of peace she felt at the end. She heard a click, then everything took on a slow-motion quality. Two figures hurled themselves out from behind a building to her left and one of them pushed her hard to the ground, landing on top of her. She heard a crack, and electric pain seared through her arm. Bits of gravel flew into her eyes and stung so badly she nearly screamed. Gunshots were fired. More footsteps pounded over the ground. She couldn't see what was going on but shouting started; all the voices were urgent and loud. More shots ruptured the night air, as loud as fireworks.

'Get down! I said get down! Lie on your front with your arms and legs spread out. Do it now!' A man's voice she didn't recognise.

'Immediate backup, all available units now,' shouted another voice.

More footsteps, more shouting. A cacophony of sirens, so many it sounded like an entire fleet was approaching. Screeching tyres. The man on top of her didn't move, and she became aware of a wetness soaking through her clothes. Had she been shot after all? What was going on?

She lay still in the agonising position, her body crushed and aching – her arm bent at an unnatural angle – for what seemed like hours. Then the voices became calmer. The frantic chaos had ended.

'He's been shot, call the paramedics over here,' someone said. Slowly, the weight on her was lifted and dragged off. She propelled herself up carefully with her good arm, and a hand was thrust towards her. She looked up to inspect its owner.

'Hello, my dear, are you all right?' It was a strong-looking man with a weather-beaten face. 'I'm Detective Jason Norton, and I've just arrested the two men who were attacking you. Please, let me help you up.'

Sister Veronica staggered to her feet, breathing heavily. The detective put his arm round her waist, but even so, she wobbled, unsteady on her feet. She looked about her, an intense pain shooting from her elbow up and down her arm. Blue-and-white lights were flashing all around her, lighting up the dark night sky. Numerous police cars and two ambulances were parked at different angles around the wasteland. Uniformed policemen and plainly-dressed ones were talking to firearms officers. Several officers were pushing two men – one of them Father John – into the back of a van. A group of paramedics were bending over a man on the floor. There was a pool of blood next to his chest. She stared at his head.

'All the saints in heaven! Isn't that Father Adams? The young priest who was always with Father Mathers?'

'Well, right man, wrong name. His name is actually David Brittan, he's one of our youngest undercover officers. We had an eye on Zachary Mathers for quite some time, and had intelligence that he could lead us to a much bigger ring of corruption. David infiltrated Mathers' life, and we were able to gather a great deal of leads.'

'But Father Mathers is dead.' Sister Veronica's voice was weak.

'Yes, unfortunately, recent events took a rather rapid turn. Mathers had got himself involved too deeply with a crime network that overlapped with the Vatican network. Sadly for him he had the greed but not the intelligence to carry it off, and we believe he was silenced before he turned out to be the weakest link and ruined things for the others involved. Sister, your arm looks broken, we need to get a paramedic to take a look at it. I'm not an expert, but I expect you'll need that reset and wrapped in plaster.'

'But what about Father Adams, or David, or whoever he really is?' Sister Veronica stared at the man on the floor. 'He was the one who threw himself on top of me, isn't he? He saved my life.'

'Yes it was him, but don't you worry, David's going to be fine.' Detective Norton gently turned her round and guided her towards an ambulance. 'I've chatted with the paramedics, luckily the bullet missed his vital organs and went straight through the soft tissue on his shoulder. They stemmed the bleeding in time, and after a few days of bed rest he'll be feeling much better. Come on, let's get you seen to now.'

'Father John?' The words caused her immense pain to say. The heartbreak caused by losing a formerly trusted friend was excruciating.

'Safely locked up and guarded in the van with his accomplice, Darius Greene. We've been watching him for weeks, thanks to the intelligence we picked up. That's how we arrived here before anything too nasty happened, although I'll admit it was a close call, a bit too close for comfort, in fact. Don't you worry, we're going to make sure that he won't go anywhere other than prison for a very long time.'

Sister Veronica allowed herself to be guided towards the ambulance. After lying face down in gravel, her eyes stung and her vision was blurred. Her arm hurt with a pain so bad it made her want to cry. The adrenaline of the last few days was ebbing away fast; a deep fatigue replacing it. Behind the ambulance was the van containing her abductor and his accomplice. She turned her head away, never wanting to set eyes on Father John or his personal thug ever again. She wondered if she would ever heal from such a deep betrayal of friendship. Her heart, heavy already, heaved an aching sigh and she closed her eyes.

'Right, love, let's get you sat down on the bed for a minute,' the cheerful paramedic was saying. 'That's right, lean back and make yourself comfortable. I just need to roll your sleeve up and take a look at your arm.'

Sister Veronica sank back on the narrow ambulance stretcher that she was directed to, her head sinking against the thin pillow, and in seconds was swathed in the darkness of deep sleep.

47

'We're here.' Melissa craned her neck, staring through the taxi window, trying to spot the hospital entrance. 'Which ward did Sister Agnes say she was on?'

'Er, I think it was Ward 24.'

Fifteen minutes later, they'd navigated the complex network of hospital passages, floors, lifts and stairs and were buzzed into Ward 24 by a tired-looking nurse.

'You're lucky.' The nurse smiled. 'They're letting you in well after visiting hours. Special orders.'

'Bloody hell,' Melissa whispered, as they spotted Sister Veronica sitting up in bed. Next to her, prone in the hospital chair like a Gothic heroine, was Mother Superior – Sister Julia Augusta – a rosary clutched in her hands. 'Droopy drawers beat us to it.'

'We're all doomed,' Mother Superior announced lethargically to Melissa, as she bent down to kiss Sister Veronica's head. 'First, Sister Maria ran off with that errant priest–'

'I keep telling you, he's a police officer, not a priest!' Sister Veronica said loudly.

'She's not the only one leaving the cloth for love,' Bishop Hammett whispered to Melissa as she stood up. She bit her lip, grinning.

'Then Sister Veronica is almost killed,' Mother Superior went on mournfully. 'It's the devil at work, you mark my words. He'll get all of us in the end. *That ancient serpent, who is called the devil and Satan, the deceiver of the whole world.*'

'Revelation, chapter twelve, verses seven to nine,' Sister Veronica murmured.

'Sounds more like *The Exorcist* if you ask me.' Melissa stroked her friend's hair gently.

'Well, I'm sure it will all seem much brighter tomorrow,' Bishop Hammett said cheerfully. 'Now, Mother Superior, why don't you and I go and find some tea for everyone and let these ladies have a chat. They've got a lot to catch up on.'

After much persuasion and a promise of a piece of chocolate cake from the twenty-four-hour hospital café, Mother Superior allowed herself to be led away, rosary hanging languidly from one hand. Melissa sat down on the side of the bed, leant forward and gave her friend a huge bear hug.

'You are the strongest woman I know,' she said in her ear. 'And I'm proud to call you my friend, Sister. You're a real survivor.'

'You're not so bad yourself.' Sister Veronica's voice was gruff, and when Melissa pulled back, she could see tears glistening in the nun's eyes. 'Thank goodness he got Mother Superior to go, I could feel her tragicness catapulting me into a deep depression.'

Melissa grinned.

For the next ten minutes the two filled each other in on the last few hours' events. After listening in rapt horror to the account of her capture and rescue, and being shocked and speechless at the betrayal of Father John, Melissa was able to give her friend a piece of good news. Chris's contacts in Rome had found Father Bianchi sitting up in bed and well on the mend, very pleased indeed to hear that Sister Veronica was alive and well, although obviously horrified to hear she'd been through yet another ordeal. They agreed that in the morning, Melissa would send Father Bianchi some chocolates and flowers with a note of thanks, and put Sister Veronica's name on the card.

Then silence fell as the enormity of what had happened was re-evaluated, mulled over and digested, broken only by Sister Veronica's continuous position-shifting. Thoughts were constantly moving in her head too; she just couldn't seem to get a handle on the events of the last few days. So much had changed, so many new understandings were dawning. And in the most uncomfortable way, a veil had been pulled back to reveal an underbelly of Catholicism she'd had no idea existed. And it was gruesome to have to look the truth in the face. No wonder so many Catholics don't want to hear about troubles in the church, she reflected. It's so much easier to live in blind ignorance, and to put these priests, bishops and cardinals on the pedestals we need. We think we have to have some Catholic superhumans to look up to, who are somehow imbued with special religious powers. We believe that they are pure beings, in fact we believe what we are told to. But it seems they're as human and flawed as the rest of us. And once we start seeing the corruption, we can't turn a blind eye to it. Because that's insulting to the people these men and women of the cloth are hurting through their lust for power, prestige and money. Of course, not all of us in the church are corrupt, but a few are and woe betide any of us who ignore that, just because it makes our own little lives easier. Even someone who I once counted as a close friend is a wolf in sheep's clothing. How well do we really know anybody? How many more people will they hurt before something big changes? So much for the vows. It turns out chastity isn't collectively happening at all.

'Are you in pain, Sister? Would you like me to get the nurse?' Melissa looked at the old nun's arm anxiously as she shifted again. It was now rigidly ensconced in a plaster-of-Paris bandage like a large white drainpipe bent at a right angle.

'I'll be all right for a bit,' Sister Veronica said. 'It does throb though. My dear, I am very conscious that throughout our escapades we never found anything out about your own parentage.' Poor Melissa, she thought. Spending all this time chasing around Europe with me but having nothing to show for it herself.

'Oh, I don't want to know anymore.' Melissa sighed. 'What's happened has happened and I can't do anything to change that now. I want to enjoy the present and the future now, not keep worrying about the past and my birth mother. If the last week's events have taught me anything, it's to concentrate on the good in my life, and not give attention to the negative stuff. If I'm ever meant to meet her, then I will, but I'm not going to worry about it anymore.'

'That's very wise indeed.' Sister Veronica nodded approvingly. 'Listen, I keep meaning to ask you; have you heard anything from that editor chap from the paper that you mentioned?'

'Oh yes.' Melissa shot her a gleaming smile. 'I wrote the piece up while we were waiting to hear news of you; I needed something to keep me busy or I would have gone mad. I kind of figured that the world needed to know the truth, and if I could do anything to help you while I felt so helpless and had no idea where you were, then this was it. I wrote the final piece on my tablet on the way over here, after Sister Agnes told Chris about you being kidnapped by Father John. Then I emailed it to Ethan just before we arrived, and he's texted to say he's received it, so keep an eye out for the headlines tomorrow. Honestly, you couldn't make this stuff up. It's more sensational than the Christmas episode of *EastEnders*.'

Sister Veronica leant back, a faraway look in her eyes. Could this whole affair really be drawing to a close?

'Thank you,' she said. A single tear rolled down her cheek.

48

' " Absolutely Disgusting": Roman Catholic Priest accused of Murdering Own Son in London,' Sister Veronica read, chewing her toast slowly. '*Armed police were called to an abandoned industrial site in Battersea, South London, last night, where Father John McGinty was apprehended by firearms officers after a struggle. Police say he intended to murder Sister Veronica Angelica (from the Christian Heart Convent, Soho), to silence her, after she discovered he had murdered his own biological son, James Markham, and a Sister from her own order, Sr Anastasia Trehern. Sister Veronica was treated in hospital for minor injuries following the incident, but is expected to make a full recovery.*'

'Minor injuries indeed.' Sister Veronica shifted her aching arm. She read on.

'*Bishop Sabell, acting as spokesperson from the Archbishop's House in Westminster, called Father John's actions "absolutely disgusting", and said that the Roman Catholic Church, particularly in his diocese in Westminster, was doing everything they could to co-operate with police at this time.*' Sister Veronica raised her eyes to stare at Melissa, who shook her head sorrowfully.

'I'm so sorry, Sister,' Melissa said. 'Ethan said there was

nothing he could do; the story was taken out of his hands at the last minute and rewritten by the highest-ranking editor at the paper. Someone high up in the church must be manipulating this, but they had so much power Ethan was completely removed from having anything further to do with it.'

Sister Veronica sighed, brushing a pile of crumbs off the bed, half-heartedly wondering if the nurse would bring her more toast if she asked her very politely.

'That doesn't surprise me in the least,' she said eventually. 'You and Ethan did everything you could to get the story opened up for the public to read, and I thank you for that from the bottom of my heart. But this web of corruption clearly runs too deeply throughout the church and the media to have such lowly life forms like you or I make a dent in it.'

'Now listen, Sister,' Melissa said fiercely, leaning forward and taking her hands. 'Don't you *dare* lose heart. We HAVE made an impact on this. YOU'VE made an impact, can't you see? Jamie's murder wouldn't have come to light at all in the press if it hadn't been for you. You've helped to open up a secretive world – the world of biological priests' children – that the public doesn't know about. Yes, okay, so someone in the church is manipulating the content of the story, and pretending that the Catholic authorities have been supportive of the police investigation all along. They've taken out most of the detail that I wrote and made the church sound amazingly good and pious as per usual. But the bare bones of truth are there, that Father John murdered his own son. And remember, the national and international stories are always mirrored in the local, so more people than you realise will get to hear about it. This kind of truth versus censoring is going on all over the world. And hey, no one said this was going to be easy.'

'When did you become so wise?' Sister Veronica blinked, surprised. This girl was really something special; she was realising this more and more. And actually, although she'd lost one friend in Father John, she'd gained another in this exotic, wonderful journalist.

'Oh, I have my moments.' Melissa grinned. 'This is not my first rodeo with the press, Sister. Anyway, listen,' she went on, a hint of a smile playing round her lips. 'Read on if you want a real surprise.'

Sister Veronica, feeling humbled but happier, cast her tired eyes down to the newspaper again.

'*In further developments, police led the disgraced Cardinal Charles Moore away from the Archbishop's House in handcuffs early this morning. Bishop Henri Sabell, who has temporarily taken over the Cardinal's main duties, told reporters: "It has come as a total shock to us all to hear of the Cardinal's embezzlement of Vatican money. Cardinal Moore has always been a trusted friend, colleague and man of God, and we are greatly saddened to hear of his fall from grace. He and his family will be in our prayers. I know our loyal flock in the United Kingdom will quite rightly be very hurt and troubled by today's events, after learning that two of their popular leaders, Cardinal Moore and Father John, chose to follow the wrong paths. These men have unwittingly chosen roads towards hate and destruction, and in doing so turned their backs on the light of God and the road to eternal salvation. But I would like to take this opportunity to reassure our flock – both here and around the world – that these two are but unnatural bad apples in a harvest of purity. I ask our followers to focus on the fact that we have rid ourselves of their evil now, and we will continue our good work in spreading the word of God".*' Sister Veronica briefly raised her eyes to heaven. '*A spokesperson from the Vatican, Bishop Alfonsi,*' she continued reading, '*was quoted in the Vatican's words following the breaking news: "There is no excuse for this kind of secrecy and corruption in the Roman Catholic Church today. Our Pope has made that clear, has he not? We must continue to strive to be transparent in our motives and actions, and live simple, humble lives as men of God. I can confirm that the Vatican has launched its own internal investigations into how Cardinal Moore's actions and embezzlement of funds were possible, but I can say no more about it at this time, other than he was acting alone and no one else appears to have been involved. God Bless."*

'In other news, two members of a London parish council have been arrested in connection with the murder of Father Zachary Mathers. A possible link between deceased Father Mathers' misuse of council funds and Cardinal Moore's activities is being investigated...

'And so the rot grows deeper.' Sister Veronica folded the paper in half and pushed it away from her. 'Cardinal Moore is a bad man, but he is clearly being made a scapegoat for the ring of Catholic embezzlers around the world that we heard about. They must have thought he was a weak link. I'm surprised they didn't link him with the cover-up of Jamie's murder.'

'Ah, but don't forget, Sister, how the minimising of scandal is important for the church. They've said just enough in public, but not too much.' Melissa's face was grim.

'Melissa, I do believe you're becoming cynical in your old age.' Sister Veronica felt a full-bodied smile flash across her face. It felt good to smile again.

'Oh, I've always been cynical, Sister,' Melissa said, shooting a grin back at her. 'I think recent events have caused you to become just as sceptical as me. For very good reasons.'

'Yes, perhaps you're right.' Sister Veronica shifted position to stare out of the high hospital window. 'But I can't let that kind of darkness take me over. I just know there's more important things in life than corruption, murder and heinous liars.'

'What, do you mean things like love?' Melissa sat up a little straighter and tucked her hair behind her ears as Bishop Hammett walked in.

'Yes, love,' Sister Veronica mused. 'Thank you for reminding me.' She rubbed her forehead and turned her head away, the pain of John's betrayal still doing more damage than any physical injury could. At least Jamie can be laid to rest properly now, she thought. I've done my job there, helped a fellow child of a priest – God rest his soul – and the truth eventually won over evil, and my own demons have found an ounce of closure. But there's so much more dishonesty out there, this world of ours has got everything topsy-turvy; we live amid other people's lies and illusions and are expected to believe they're real.

She could still feel Bishop Alfonsi's cruel eyes boring into her, the image kept replaying in her mind, taunting her like a stuck photo reel. He would have snuffed her life out without a second thought, she was quite sure of it. Was probably kicking himself for not finishing the job. And he had got off scot-free, no repercussions or being held to account for him; just like the other criminals and embezzlers who had used Cardinal Moore as their scapegoat. How was this fair? How was it possible in the modern world? And John did his best to end her once and for all, and now he would be languishing in prison for the murders of his son and Sister Anastasia, probably for the rest of his life. And Zachary Mathers was dead; even though she'd despised the man, she couldn't help feeling that although he'd thought he was a king in the game of power, he'd actually been a pawn, used and abused and finally snuffed out by those who were even more greedy than him. Nothing made sense anymore. There was too much duplicity and duality in the world, it made her head hurt.

Well, that's it. I'm never getting involved in anything like this again, Sister Veronica thought, in case anyone was listening. Oh no. A quiet life for me from now on, thank you *very* much.

49

'Henri?' Cardinal Moore's hand shook as he grasped the receiver. 'Why is this happening?' The Central London police station was cold and bare; his cell even worse, the officers professional but distant. And he was being treated like a nobody, like an invisible Joe Bloggs. Allowed one phone call, he'd turned to his most trusted friend.

'I really don't know, Charles, it's so unfair.' Bishop Henri Sabell's tones were smooth yet sympathetic. Ensconced in the Archbishop's comfortable office, he inspected his nails and tapped his expensively-shod foot. His new shoes needed wearing in a bit.

'But it wasn't just *me*. It wasn't only me, Henri, you know that, you witnessed others in the Vatican, there were lots of us in on the scheme.' Cardinal Moore sank to the floor, dragging the receiver and wire with him. His thoughts were splintering, fragmenting; he had not known it was possible for mere thinking to physically hurt. All this had something to do with that bloody bitch of a woman, Sister Veronica. If her repeated escapes hadn't made him look so incompetent... It was beyond irksome that she was still alive. All his excellent work with the

218

assessors was now redundant, futile. The emotion of hatred was truly a powerful one. He had lost everything. *Everything.* 'Matteo. Bishop Alfonsi. They've framed me for some reason. But why, Henri? Why?'

Henri gave a deep sigh, wondering what the correct thing to say to the Cardinal would be. Of course, he'd helped Matteo set Charles up; it was the only possible thing to do, given the Cardinal's blinkered narcissistic tendencies and the mess he'd got himself into. Put one end in Rome in touch with media in the UK, and suggest a few things they needed to say. And it had been absolutely necessary to keep his own name out of the press in connection to the goings-on with Jamie Markham; no point in involving more people than were necessary where that debacle was concerned. And he intended to move the church and the country – and, of course, his own career – forward. Unfortunately, Charles didn't really have the wit or understanding to thrive in that atmosphere of high intelligence at the Vatican; he was too idealistic, he really believed every word people told him. Of course, Matteo hadn't tampered with the priest's children's document when Charles had asked him to, which was a shame because the old goat, Sister Veronica, had managed to get hold of Father John's name from Father Bianchi as a result. But the Vatican fathers had already decided Charles needed to be pushed out by then. It was a real shame that Father John had been caught – an affair that had nothing to do with him, Henri Sabell – he had liked, admired and revered the high intelligence and quiet guile of the man, as many had. But his demise just showed that one couldn't be too careful.

He, Henri, could see that there was a shelf life for thinkers like Charles. To not only survive, but to thrive in the inner circle of Vatican intellectuals, one had to have a more creative psychological approach; to have more wits and keen mercurial reactionary ability. There was no point explaining this to

Charles, because the poor thing simply wouldn't understand. The only thing he could do at this point was to make soothing noises and offer condolences. Then go out and reap his rewards.

'I absolutely understand how you feel, Charles,' Henri said, flicking his arm until his sleeve rode up, revealing the time on his watch. It had been a great honour to have been asked to take over Father John's position as head contact for the monetary exchanges in the United Kingdom. It had been Archbishop Cancio himself who'd phoned, which was a huge honour. It showed how much he was trusted, and he wasn't going to let his good friends in the Vatican City down. 'It all must feel so completely unexpected and unfair.'

'Oh, Henri.' Cardinal Moore closed his eyes. 'I knew I could count on you.'

'Yes, indeed you can, Charles.' Henri Sabell smiled. 'I'm flying to Rome this weekend in order to tie up some loose ends, in fact.'

'What loose ends? What do you mean, Henri?'

'I simply mean I'm going there to try to get to the bottom of who did what to you,' Bishop Sabell said, his tones smoother than velvet.

'Thank you, Henri. I know you'll set this all right.'

'Oh indeed I will, Charles. Now I'm afraid I must go, or I'll be late for a rather important meeting.'

'Who with?'

But the line was already dead.

50

Sister Veronica sat silently, watching a fat pigeon walking up and down the window ledge. She would be going home this afternoon, back to the Convent of the Christian Heart; back to her little bedroom with its piles of papers, books, pens and knick-knacks. A return to normality. The only problem was, she no longer knew what normality was. And she wasn't sure she wanted to go back to the convent in Soho; too much had changed and she wasn't sure she belonged there, or anywhere else for that matter.

Her time in hospital had been a reprieve, especially with the privilege of being given her own room in which to recuperate. The kind nurses who brought her tea and checked her blood pressure seemed like overworked angels; always ready with kind words or smiles. The only slight complaint she had was that the hospital didn't appear to stock custard cream biscuits, and it had been so long since she'd tasted one.

On the plus side, the weather was cooling at last, which made everything more comfortable. But her insides felt strange when she considered her return to the convent. She felt self-conscious, embarrassed almost. She'd been an errant nun on a detective mission to solve a murder. For goodness' sake, Sister Irene would have a field day with that one, she'd dine out on it for eternity and never let her hear the end of it. So much had changed over the last few days; *she* had fundamentally altered, metamorphosing from an unknower into one saturated with too much knowledge about the corruption in the institution of which she was part. It was all so disillusioning. She could no longer trot down to mass and pray with the other sisters with a naïve heart. She could no longer listen to her comrades rattle on about how wonderful those at the Vatican were during mealtimes, now that she knew the extent of hypocrisy and venality that spread through the underworld of Catholicism like a cancer. It was all too much. Perhaps she should look into a transfer after all.

Melissa and Chris – she could no longer call him Bishop Hammett now steps were finally being initiated for him to leave the priesthood – were enjoying the first flush of love; wrapped up together in their little bubble and no longer visiting her so much now she was truly on the mend. Of course, she was fine with that, of *course* she was. The very idea that she was jealous of the love and intimacy they'd found was ludicrous; she wouldn't even entertain such an outlandish notion for one second. There was no way she was feeling lonely, she never had and she never would. The indignation of it caused her to sit up straighter in bed with such force that the pigeon turned to stare.

Sister Veronica found herself fantasising about moving to a tiny isolated cottage overlooking the sea, and living out her days in glorious, hermit-like isolation. She let her eyelids droop, the complete lack of motivation that had overtaken her body since finding out the duplicity of Father John, still dumbing down her thoughts and mood. Everything seemed rather empty. Although, she reminded herself sternly, she still had so much to be thankful for, like her good friends Agnes and Melissa. Now don't start getting maudlin, Veronica, or you'll end up like Mother Superior, and what a turn of events that would be.

Her thoughts were interrupted by slow, laboured footsteps in the corridor outside. She looked up.

'Hello, Veronica?' Sister Agnes Claire's face peeped round the door. A large explosion of warmth erupted in Sister Veronica at the sight of her friend. 'Is it okay if I come in?'

'Yes of course, please do,' Sister Veronica said with a huge smile. She shifted up in bed and patted the chair next to her. 'How lovely to see you, Agnes. I didn't think I would have any visitors today. You know I'm coming back to the convent at some point this afternoon?'

'Ah yes,' Sister Agnes said, surveying her friend's eyes. 'It's awful to see you suffering like this, I've felt so useless these past few days not being able to do anything to help you.' Sitting down carefully in the chair, her face wincing with the expected arthritic twinges of pain, Sister Agnes placed a bumper-sized pack of custard cream biscuits on the bed. 'That's rather why I slipped away to visit you. Needed to have a quiet word.'

Sister Veronica, about to rip open the custard creams, stopped and looked at her friend.

'Why?' she asked. 'What's happened?'

'Oh, well. I'm still not sure I should bother you with this.' Sister Agnes' forehead wrinkled in faux concern. 'I know you've been through such a lot and I don't want to burden you with more stress.'

'Agnes, you tell me this instant!' The old fire returned to Sister Veronica's voice. 'I've been sitting in bed for two days now, with nothing better to do than stare at the wall or watch that ridiculous pigeon out there. I'm feeling completely fine, and I'm not stressed in the least. Now if you need my help with something, let's hear it.'

'Oh well, if you're sure,' Sister Agnes said. 'It's just that something very out of the ordinary happened last night, and none of us are sure what to do.'

'Well get on with it, Agnes, stop dilly-dallying.' Sister Veronica leaned forward, her eyes bright.

'A tiny baby was left on the doorstep of the convent,' Sister Agnes said. 'Just dumped there like a shopping delivery, can you believe it? She was all wrapped up in dirty blankets, lying quietly in a cardboard box, her big eyes staring up like saucers.'

'Who found her?'

'Mother Superior.' Sister Agnes suppressed a smile. 'She's taken to her bed today, of course, can't cope. Says the world is ending now that babies are being abandoned on doorsteps.'

'Surely you would phone the police, Agnes?' Sister Veronica looked at her friend, feeling puzzled. 'Isn't that obvious? Or an ambulance – if the baby is unwell, or even social services?'

'Well' – Sister Agnes leaned further forward conspiratorially – 'things are a bit more complicated than that, I'm afraid, Veronica. Because there were two things placed on top of the baby's chest, tucked under the blanket so they wouldn't fly away in the breeze. One was a tarot card. And the other was a note that simply said, *Take me to Sister Catherine*.'

Sister Veronica exhaled, aware that her heart was beating faster.

'What was on the tarot card, Agnes? What was the image?'

'Oh, it was awful to see.' A pained look clouded Sister Agnes' eyes. 'Lying there, on top of this beautiful baby girl – who can't be more than two months old – was a card full of savage images; a burning tower, fighting, dead bodies, and the most gruesome maimed head covered in blood. Underneath the image it had one word, *Destruction*.'

'Right!' Sister Veronica ripped her covers back with her good arm, and swung her legs over the side of the bed. 'I'm coming now, Agnes. Please find a doctor and tell them to discharge me this instant. I'll do more good helping with this at the convent than sitting around here like a useless lump, watching pigeons.' She fumbled in the locker beside her bed, pulling out her satchel.

Sister Agnes turned away, hiding a smile.

'Well, if you're sure, Veronica?' she said, making for the door. 'I'll go and find a doctor for you now.'

But Sister Veronica didn't hear, because she was humming a merry tune, aware that colour was flooding back into her world. Of course she belonged at the Convent of the Christian Heart; they wouldn't survive without her, for heaven's sake. Putting aside her packing for a minute or two, she broke the cellophane from her friend's kind gift of custard creams. A baby, a note and a tarot card? She was needed back at the convent right away, no mistake about that. Oh yes, she was a changed woman as a result of her recent experiences, but now more than ever she had a thirst for righting the wrongs done to others, even if it meant her getting into different types of trouble. She'd rather that than sit around pontificating about love and goodness but doing nothing practical to show for it. And as well as needing to sort this new mess out, a new idea for a book was being born in her mind. The addictive tug of writing, temporarily dissipated by recent horrific events, had begun again within her and it was a delightfully fizzy and reinvigorating feeling. But there was always time for just one biscuit first... maybe two...

THE END

ACKNOWLEDGEMENTS

There are many people I would like to thank for their help and support with bringing The Convent to life.

Firstly, Betsy Reavley for believing in Sister Veronica, and giving her the opportunity to step out in to the wide, public world. Also Ian Skewis, for his incredible, incisive editing. And Tara Lyons and everyone else at Bloodhound Books who work tirelessly to enable the publication and marketing processes to happen.

My mum, Sue, for generally being amazing. And my wonderful partner Rich, for his unending support with my writing. And of course my super star children, Bethan, Olivia and Ben; always shine your light brightly you gorgeous human beings. And my friends and family for their interest and honesty when I've floated numerous ideas past them. Thank you all!

Printed in Great Britain
by Amazon